Provision and Submission

Provision and Submission

Insight into a Black Cultural Conundrum

Chelsea Nicole Jenkins

ISBN: Softcover   978-1-6641-7561-7
             eBook   978-1-6641-7560-0

Print information available on the last page.

Rev. date: 05/19/2021

To order additional copies of this book, contact:
Xlibris
844-714-8691
www.Xlibris.com
Orders@Xlibris.com
827378

CONTENTS

Preface xi

PART 1: INTRODUCTION

Chapter 1   Decisions, Decisions 1
Chapter 2   High Hopes...9
Chapter 3   Misunderstanding vs. Reality.......................................13
Chapter 4   Millennials' Pitiful Priorities: Birkin Bags and
Game Systems 19
Chapter 5   The Benefit of the Doubt 25
Chapter 6   Love Gets No Love...29

PART 2: THE INTERVIEWS

Chapter 7   Aunyā: The Liberal Womanist 37
Chapter 8   Katrina: The Straight Shooter 43
Chapter 9   Cynthia: The Mogul in the Making..............................51
Chapter 10   Daryel: The Cool, Calm, and Collected 59
Chapter 11   Odjo: The Southern Gentleman 65
Chapter 12   Greg: The "Father First"..71
Chapter 13   Charles and Alycia—The Dutiful Dad and the
Money-Making Mom 81
Chapter 14   Chris and Val—The Loving and Laid-Back Couple 87
Chapter 15   Mike and Shak—The Two Peas in a Pod.....................91
Chapter 16   Rai and Olivia—The Linguistic and Artistic...............95

Chapter 17 Malik and Bri—The Young Love 105
Chapter 18 Fletcher and Carol—The Seasoned Love 111

PART 3: STRONG WOMEN AND SUBMISSION

Chapter 19 The Interconnectedness of Success, Provision,
            and Submission According To God's Word................ 117
Chapter 20 Submission Is Not for the Weak................................123
Chapter 21 In Conclusion 127

Sources...129

I dedicate this book to my parents, Charles and Nicole. You two are my greatest support and my biggest inspiration. I strive to make you proud, and I pray that I have so far.

I also pray that God blesses me with a love that is strong, genuine, and timeless, like the one you two share.

My brother and I have witnessed your best
moments, as well as your worst.
Yet your love is still admirable in my eyes.

Thank you for showing us what healthy, fluid provision and submission looks like between husband and wife.

Thank you for your example of real love.
Not perfect love,
but *real* love.

I love you both with all my heart.

My people are destroyed for the lack of knowledge.

—Hosea 4:6

Preface

Take a deep breath.

Trust me, you're going to need it.

Now, repeat after me: "I give myself permission to release all my harmful conceptualized beliefs. These beliefs may be prohibiting me from understanding my needs and desires and keeping me from giving or receiving a love that is pure and genuine."

Inhale. Exhale.

Now that we've gotten that taken care of, we may proceed.

When referring to romantic relationships, the words "provide" and "submit" hold a lot of weight. Immediately numerous visualizations and perceptions come to mind, and we either love them or detest them. For some folks, there's more of a gray area.

Whatever your thoughts may be, breaking down what it means to "provide" and what it means to "submit" can be a slippery slope. I've come to learn that there are many of us who would be just fine with not even opening that can of worms at all.

Like, ever.

Well, hold on tight because this book is a no-holds-barred showdown of the words "provide" and "submit." The lines have been blurred and, unfortunately, we've been combining reality with unrealistic expectation. Our negative thoughts and behaviors have proven to be the perfect recipe for doomed relationships and, ultimately, a cutthroat battle of the sexes.

We'll analyze the frustration and resentment that some of us have developed for our respective gender roles and what each of us is expected to do as men and as women.

But first, I'd like to use this moment to say that this is *not* a shady book. This is not written by one of those fire-and-brimstone Bible thumpers. This is not a book filled with condemnation. If you're expecting to be put down or belittled based off your relationship status, the choices you've made in the past, your values, your beliefs, or your current circumstances, then let me assure you once again—that is not what I'm here for. As a matter of fact, shaming you for your habits and opinions would be counterproductive to my mission.

My mission is to discuss my observations and be completely vulnerable in sharing my true stories with you.

No, this is not a journalistic novel. My unbiased and objective writing days in high school and college are over. I wrote this book to offer my opinions and describe my values regarding romance and partnership in contrast to some of our new-age cultural norms and relationship patterns. But, most importantly, I will do so by basing them off God's Word and the merit of my thorough research; I've cited each source at the end.

Plus, I've included my most striking revelations and quotes from real-life conversations with people just like you and me. I used these discussions to support my perspective and insert constructive criticism where and when it's necessary.

What I am here to do is uplift, inform, and provide wholesome, honest, raw, worldly, *and* biblical insight from my point of view. Plus, I've included the perspectives of numerous Black, heterosexual singles, couples, domestic partners, and spouses.

Part 1

Introduction

If we look back in time, we will notice a pattern, or a theme being reinforced. Within each time frame, society has reiterated the notion that women are to be submissive, to have a soft and agreeable disposition, and to ultimately surrender to the desires and directives of men. On the other hand, men are taught to be protectors, providers, and leaders, which additionally calls for a more assertive disposition in contrast to women.

Don't believe me? That's okay. I've got receipts.

In primitive times (before Christ or BC), men were scouters. They had to travel the bitter, unforgiving terrain on foot with their wives and children. While scouting for the tribe out in the wilderness, hunting for food, and searching for the next best place of refuge, men were the lookouts. There were dangers they could encounter, including wild animals and hostile humans. To keep the women and children safe, they'd travel in single file, placing the men at the front and the rear of the line, allowing the children and women to follow along in between the men, protecting them from both ends.

Other examples are the ones that God himself set for us. The Holy Bible emphasizes clear expectations of the respective roles for men and women.

To begin with, one thing we should all agree on is, just as well as God created the heavens and the earth, God also created man and woman. Genesis 1:27 (ESV) tells us, *"So God created man in his own image; in the image of God, he created him; male and female, he created them."*

But bear in mind that Adam (man) was created by God *first.* This means, since the creation of woman came after man, God intended for men to be both intellectually and physically capable of leading women with great competence and graciousness and making wise decisions based off their discernment and foresight.

God placed Adam in the garden of Eden so he could work and tend to the plants, herbs, produce, and all the garden's flying, hopping, crawling inhabitants.

He instructed Adam that he was free to eat from any tree within the garden of Eden—all except for the tree of the knowledge of good and evil; that one was off-limits. Adam was instructed that eating from the tree of knowledge would surely cause him to die. Adam obeyed the Lord and continued to tend to the garden throughout his days.

While God was admiring how all the animals worked in pairs and groups and lived harmoniously among one another, he couldn't help but notice that Adam was alone.

So, God decided that it's only right that Adam, too, had a partner—a companion he could depend on in his time of need. Genesis 2:18 (ESV) tells us, *"Then the Lord God said, 'It is not good that the man should be alone; I will make him a helper fit for him.'"*

And with that, God placed Adam in a deep sleep and removed one of his ribs. And from the rib of Adam, God created a woman, who Adam would later name Eve.

So, there you have it! God knew that men were simply incomplete without fearfully and wonderfully made women whom they could confide in and who would contribute to their success and overall well-being.

But, of course, things soon went south.

Although Adam had instructed Eve that God said eating from the tree of knowledge was forbidden, Eve was deceived by the serpent and ate fruit from the forbidden tree anyway. To make matters worse, she was able to sway Adam to eat from the tree of knowledge as well. Once the serpent told Eve of how knowledgeable she'd be and assured her that they wouldn't die, Adam was convinced to follow the lead of his wife and take direction from her despite the Lord's instructions.

After learning of how Adam and Eve were deceived by the serpent and went against his orders, God decided on the appropriate punishment for women. In addition to women bearing painful childbirth, God also declared in Genesis 3:16, *"Your desire will be for your husband and he will rule over you."*

God's punishment for men, on the other hand, was that they must work by the sweat of their brow until the day they perish and return to the earth themselves (Gen. 3:19). Then, to further enforce this commandment, God later said that any man who doesn't provide for his family has denied the faith and is worse than an infidel or a nonbeliever (1 Tim. 5:8).

God further enforced his commandments for women as well; he made this clear in Colossians 3:18 (ESV): *"Wives, submit to your husbands, as is fitting in the Lord."*

So here we are—cursed to this day due to the decision of Eve, who overstepped her boundaries and exercised ill authority over her husband. Then there was Adam, who failed at exercising his God-given obligation to lead by example, causing them both to be exiled from the garden of Eden.

Now, don't get me wrong. I understand that the Bible is an ancient book, and even though it is holy, it is still filled with rather extreme rules and customs that were normal in those days. But let's face it—many biblical and religious practices and beliefs would be quite unjust, sexist, and cruel if they were applied word for word today. In life, there are some gray areas that must be acknowledged or, at the very least, taken into consideration. I don't believe in just enforcing a black-or-white outlook to every situation. That's why it's imperative that we develop a sincere and humble understanding—*with the quickness*—between men and women and what it is that we truly need and desire from one another.

Fast-forward to the 1900s. We began to have more qualitative and quantitative scholarly findings available to us regarding the behaviors and expectations of men and women. Doctors, psychologists, and educators were able to conduct research and present information based off their observations.

Alice H. Eagly, a noteworthy professor of psychology, is responsible for the studies in 1987 that birthed the social role theory. This theory argues that widely shared gender stereotypes were created due to the division of labor, which characterizes a society. Historically, in Western societies, more men worked in order to earn money within positions of high authority and status. On the other hand, the small number of assignments left went to women. These assignments focused more on showing affection, being attentive to others, and taking care of them—both physically and psychologically.

So, it should come as no surprise how the nuances of these roles further perpetuated the association of men with agency—to provide a service or facilitate transactions—and women with work that focused more on communion—tending to the needs and thoughts or sharing intimacy with others.

African American men and women have especially held true to these gender norms or narratives. We've gone from specific ideologies and following gender norms without question within our culture to creating a new status quo; one that we can't seem to see eye to eye on. Therefore, it's been causing divisiveness within our relationships.

Chapter 1

Decisions, Decisions

According to "Married Black Men's Opinions as to Why Black Women Are Disproportionately Single: A Qualitative Study," Black women are provided with messages about romantic relationships by not only their elders but also their communities. This notion was confirmed by women counseled in clinical settings regarding these issues. These women confirmed their uncertainties about the permanency of marriage in addition to their preference for focusing on their professional desires and obligations.

As a single Black woman in her mid-twenties, I can attest to the dueling pertinence of independence and career stability versus the equally deep-rooted value of finding a "good husband."

Speaking in terms of the ideologies that Black women are administered, Boyd-Franklin and Boyd wrote in 1998:

"One is a message of independence (e.g., 'God bless the child who has her own') with its implication that Black men cannot be trusted to stay with and provide for women. The other is a message that a woman's utmost goal is to find a Black man who will take care of her."

Furthermore, these contradictory messages can surely be attributed to Black women's decisions to not form these romantic relationships at all, or if they do engage in these romantic relationships with Black men, they experience great difficulties.

But still, I can't help but wonder if it's not just the way we choose to be as "strong" Black women. In fact, I sometimes wonder if some Black women's tendency to become workaholics—focused solely on earning an education, wealth, and a stable career—is actually a coping mechanism.

Well, okay—how about I speak for myself and you decide whether you can relate or not? I'll be the first to admit that I fantasize about becoming a loving wife and mother quite often. I've told my mom multiple times that I feel as though God put me on this earth to become a wife and a mother, if nothing else. I've always felt maternal and the urge to live a loving, wholesome, family-oriented lifestyle.

However, true love and a partnership both serve as prerequisites to that monogamous life that I dream of, which becomes more and more elusive the older I get and the more complex my relationships become.

My mom had a particular rhetoric in reference to her ideal sequence of my life: "Chelsea already knows, she better not bring home any babies or any baby daddies before she brings me a degree. And even after she earns her degree, I'ma need her to land a stable career. *Then* we can worry about her getting a [Godly] husband and starting a family."

Those words stuck to me in a more effective way than she probably expected. With every romantic heartbreak, rejection, or letdown, I remembered my mom's words—mainly because these romantic disasters were happening with every educational, career, and financial accomplishment I'd reached.

I'd landed an amazing scholarship at an award-winning news station. I'd made the dean's list and graduated from a private university. After graduating, I subsequently financed a brand-new car for myself, self-published two poetry books, and landed an entry-level job—my first salaried position—at a multibillion-dollar corporation, then moved out of my parents' home and began leasing my own apartment.

Now I say this with the utmost humility—even after all those accomplishments, I knew I was just getting started.

Sure, I was upset and distraught over this guy or that one. But there was one thing that they couldn't take from me—my independence. I prided myself on the fact that, no matter how much I may have *wanted* a man, I knew my mom and dad taught me well enough to *never need* one. But I couldn't deny that the desire of having a solid man by my side was the strongest feeling I'd ever experienced, especially whenever I witnessed my acquaintances fall in love, move in with their partner, get engaged, and have babies (in no particular order).

Instead of finding true love, I was writing business plans and coordinating book signings. When everyone else was moving in with their partners, I'd found myself moving *back in* with my parents in order to save more money for my big move to another city—on my own. While women I knew were going into labor, I was birthing what I knew in my heart would be my biggest project yet—the social study that would become my third book.

I had to learn to trust God's timing. I felt so confused, excited, and liberated all at once, so I didn't quite know what to make of it. In the midst of one of the biggest transitional stages of my life, my favorite Bible verse is what kept me encouraged.

Proverbs 3:5–6 (NIV): *"Trust in the Lord with all your heart and lean not unto your own understanding; In all your ways, submit to him, and he will make your paths straight."*

So, there it was. My mother had always instilled in me the desire to focus on my education and my entrepreneurial endeavors before being wrapped up in finding a man—not at all in an overbearing or condescending way, but she did believe in nurturing me as her child while still "keepin' it real," as she would say. All in all, her thing was, men aren't going anywhere. Men will always be here, and God will unite me with my man in his perfect time, so I should work toward my goals and build my own bank account in the meantime.

While that's all true, it's also thanks to my mother and father how I understood early on what the real essence of provision and submission between husband and wife looks like. My parents met when they were just nineteen and twenty years old. Not long after they met, my mother gave birth to my brother, and two years later, they were married. Yep, they're still married to this day—twenty-eight years and counting.

Both of my parents are business owners and have been for over twenty-five years collectively. I watched my father earn an honest living my whole life. He's a certified HVAC technician and works hard every day. He makes sure his family is protected and cared for—both financially and physically. My mother is a hard worker as well. She's opened her own financial agency. A busybody, she is always on the go—at an appointment or on her way to the next one. Although she often gave my father leeway so he could have a major influence in the decision process regarding our family, they still demonstrated how they were a team.

Our parents showed me and my older brother that provision and submission is fluid. Because of the positive example they set, I never concocted any negative perspective for either role. And I know that this is truly a privilege and a blessing, which humbles me.

As a child, I saw my parents as nothing more than two people who, though they may not have always seen eye to eye, knew they were still on the same team, and they loved each other more than anything. Therefore, I too looked forward to a love and partnership of my own from a young age.

And I was determined to have just that.

I was twenty-four years old. It was my first time catching a flight alone.

All in the name of love, or so I thought—or so I hoped.

After my layover, I boarded the flight to my final destination: Washington, D.C. I had decided to go and visit my seven-year situationship while he was in school, earning his Doctorates. After rekindling our communication for the umpteenth time, I was complaining to him, saying that I needed a breath of fresh air, and I told him I was planning on "running away" and taking a quick vacation. So, he suggested that I come and visit him.

He sent me money to help pay for my flight and a hotel, and I was on my way.

I figured that would be the perfect time to really try to get through to him. I was nervous because I was contemplating *how* I was going to finally get an answer out of him—without making it awkward or starting an argument.

"Look, I love you. I see potential in all that we could be. Do you want me or not?"

Easier thought than said. Although I tried multiple times to be gracious and understanding and to calmly verbalize how I was ready for us to become exclusive, there was no use. Then I told him at the very least, I wanted to keep in contact on a more consistent basis and continue to strengthen our bond as friends. Of course, I had faith of us becoming more when the time was right. I loved him. And even though he never said it, when we were together, he made me feel like he loved me, too. Even if he did love me, I still could never get through to him how the lack of communication was hurting me. My words always seemed to go in one ear and out the other.

I felt like I was on an emotional rollercoaster. Every now and then I'd block his number or ignore him. I was trying to avoid the feeling of being manipulated whenever he'd contact me when I least expected it. Either way, it didn't matter; I felt miserable with him and even more miserable without him.

Truth be told, I was happy for him! I admired him for doing the hard work and furthering his education. I guess I just felt forgotten and unimportant with all the distance and uncertainty.

Okay, back to my flight.

After my layover, once I got to my seat, a friendly middle-aged white man sat next to me and made my acquaintance for the next hour or so before we reached DC. After telling me about how he was an accomplished real estate agent who was traveling on business, I told him I was a college grad and an author. He asked me if I was traveling for business or to visit family. I looked at him and said, "No, I'm just visiting a friend. He's away at college."

He paused for a moment and gave me a solemn look. "Now is this really just a friend? Or is he more than a friend?"

I chuckled, taken aback by the straightforward inquiry that made a million thoughts and fears run through my mind. "Well, we are really close and have been for years. But since we're far apart, we're not in an exclusive relationship. But we do care a lot about each other and want to keep in touch."

I found myself almost overexplaining and trying to make it make sense to a perfect stranger.

"Ah, I see." He nodded. "Well, I hope everything works out well for you both."

For the longest, I'd hoped so too, but eventually, I accepted the fact that maybe God had other plans for us both and its best to just move forward with my life and let him do the same. I figured everything'll come full circle, soon.

Some of you may be saying, "Okay, so what in the world does this sob story have anything to do with the topic of provision and submission?"

Don't worry! I was just getting there.

"Provision" in relationships is about having a plan for yourself *and* your significant other, right? Right.

I never doubted my friend's capability of being a good provider. He's intelligent and going into a lucrative field. I never doubted his capability of being a man and being mature and responsible. Most importantly, I never doubted my willingness to submit to him and his plans or desires for us if he were to ever confess his love for me and *ask* that I put my trust in him.

But that was the thing—what I *did* doubt was his desire for the both of us to build *together*. Whenever I spoke of the future, success, or a family, his responses were always the same:

"I can see you doing that."

"I can see you living in that city."

"For my birthday, I was thinking that me and my homeboys should link up out of town."

"I'll go wherever the money is, but I'm still not sure where I want to live after I graduate."

The bottom line is that he never once spoke of "us." *His* plans were to provide for *himself,* not *us.*

His plans were to make memories with his friends and others that he cared about, *not with me.*

My point is not to vilify him. The fact that he didn't want to be with me does not make him a bad person.

However, it took almost eight years for me to realize that he simply did not want to be with me, and my healthy understanding of provision and submission was irrelevant if I remained in that one-sided situation.

Have you ever cut yourself off from someone while you still had a lot of love for them, because you knew it was for your own good?

I have.

To this day, I wish my friend the best and I pray that he receives everything he worked so hard for.

Chapter 2

High Hopes

So just in case I haven't made it clear by now, I have never been lucky in love. I'm still not convinced that I've met my soul mate just yet. Be that as it may, I still *love* love! I'm not only intrigued by love, but it also seems like such a worthy and blissful destination. My mom often refers to me as a hopeless romantic. The idea of love moves me. Out of everyone I know, I'm the mushiest. But the bottom line is, although I'm enamored with the thought of love, I don't believe I've ever experienced true, mutual love for myself, which—I can't lie—kind of gets me down every now and then.

Women especially suffer from a stigma attached to us—how we should be wed and have children before thirty or we've neglected staying within the parameters of our biological clocks.

To be completely honest, it didn't really dawn on me until I had to find my birth certificate for the latest position I had gotten hired for. I looked and saw my mother's age at the time of my birth—twenty-five. It hit me like a ton of bricks. *Wow. Now I'm twenty-five myself. I can't imagine being someone's mom right now.* And she was *married* and with her *second child* when she was my age!

You've heard of Ella Mai, right? The rising R & B crooner from the UK? She has a song on her debut album called "Easy". From the first time I heard it, I mentally added it to my wedding playlist. (Ah-ah!

Judgement-free, remember? Some of you probably have wedding aspects planned out too and aren't even in a relationship, let alone about to get married. It's okay.) Anyhoo, the song is beautiful. The chorus says, "Love is easy, easy, so don't you make it hard."

I couldn't agree more. I hear all sorts of sayings of how, on the contrary, love is "no walk in the park" and how difficult it is to be in a relationship or to be married, especially, and how much you must sacrifice in order for things to "work." That's the thing—I don't want my love and my marriage to just "work."

What I long for is an unbreakable bond—an unmatched, incredible, almost-supernatural love. I want playfulness, spontaneity, adventure—the ultimate friendship. I want the stuff of cinematic splendor—the kind of love that you only read about. I want the kind of love that is usually portrayed through the characters and plot of a Nicholas Sparks classic.

Ordinary love "works."

What I want is something magical yet, as Ella Mai said, "easy."

That's the point I'm making. Our lack of comprehension of the terms "provision" and "submission" is part of what makes love so hard for us. It is the common enemy of young African American couples and singles. Yet it always seems to be Black men against Black women as opposed to how it should be: Black men and Black women *against the problem.*

Having a true understanding of provision and submission can help us get back to what's truly important for relationships—having respect for each other and actively valuing the importance of the greater good of the partnership.

Another driving force for my research and the entirety of this study was my desire to understand where others were coming from—even if I disagreed with them. I've never been a closed-minded woman. I realize that there are different variables and alternate perspectives that contribute to the genetic and organic makeups of our circumstances. Although we hate to admit it, we are just folks on the outside looking into the situational outcomes of another person's prerogative or their habits.

Whether it's spot-on or way off, initial perception is *everything*—especially within relationships.

"Circumstances Beyond Their Control: Black Women's Perceptions of Black Manhood" states that Black women's perception of Black men has an influence on a partnership's decisions, the quality of a relationship, health behaviors, and other aspects of personal and psychosocial well-being.

Now, in chapter 1, we already discussed how modern-day African American women who were professionally counseled in a clinical study expressed apprehension concerning the capability of some African American men to take care of them in a way that they find suitable. Some may even argue that the roles are beginning to reverse.

Given our cyclical teachings over the generations and what we're taught within our society from a young age, it's not unlikely for women to be taken care of by men. However, there's a percentage of women who are the breadwinners providing for their male partners.

Does that nugget of information make you feel uncomfortable? Does the thought of an able-bodied, mentally competent man being financially taken care of by a woman make you cringe? The reversal of roles is almost unsettling to some.

Chapter 3

Misunderstanding vs. Reality

Before we dive any deeper, let's note that gender norms or gender expectations are associated with the numerous roles of both men and women. Additionally, we have our gender schemas to thank for these expectations.

Gender schemas are mental systems of association that categorize gender beliefs, expectations, and behaviors based on whether you're a man or a woman.

Both observational learning (one's environment) and parental teachings contribute to the ideas we develop, which construct our gender schemas. Furthermore, these gender schemas and gender-role beliefs can be passed on from generation to generation.

As stated earlier, according to society, a man's role or expectation is to provide, and a woman's role or expectation is to submit.

Now, pause. I believe this is the perfect time to break down the true meanings of these terms.

For us to gain a clearer understanding, we must first know the true origins, or the etymologies, of the words "submit" and "provide."

The word "submit" is defined as *"accept or yield to a superior force or to the authority or will of another person."*

It is equally important that we acknowledge the word "authority."

"Authority" derives from the Latin word "auctor," which is "author" in modern English. The word "author" means "leader," according to the *Online Etymology Dictionary.*

Still with me? I hope so.

Conversely, the word "provide" has multiple meanings.

The first one, which comes from the *Merriam-Webster Dictionary,* is "*to supply or make available.*"

We knew that, right?

However, when speaking in terms of relationships, my favorite meaning of "provide"—and the one that is the most relevant—would be the third definition: "*to take precautionary measures.*"

Now, taking precautionary measures involves acting with foresight, correct? Taking precautionary measures helps ensure that one is thinking and planning or preparing for what could take place in the future.

You could say that a person who provides is in essence a forward-thinking individual.

Although these definitions are readily available to us on the internet, some of us still may have the tendency to see them as undesirable or old-fashioned.

The fact of the matter is the members of our generation (millennials) seem to struggle with the dueling representations of what it means to be a provider and what it means to be submissive. These dueling representations would be the *misunderstanding* versus the *reality.*

Again, let's not forget the main contributing factors to many of our misunderstandings of these roles: our upbringings—what we witnessed (or did not bear witness to) within our homes while growing up, social media—what the gossip blogs and celebrities have to say regarding relationship matters and couples' expectations, our past traumas from previous relationships (*cough cough* "*baggage*"), and society.

Just because we're falling victim to these external and internal elements, that doesn't mean we have to allow them to completely deprogram our capability to give and receive healthy love.

It's up to us to save ourselves, and I believe it starts with debunking the misunderstanding and educating ourselves and accepting reality. When we believe that a relationship is comprised of sponsorship, dictatorship, and inferiority, then we miss out on the healthy aspects of relationships, which are provision, submission, and partnership.

Misunderstanding vs. Reality

Sponsorship vs. Provision

Sponsorship says,

- *"Buy me whatever I want."*
- *"Financially maintaining my desired lifestyle is my partner's obligation."*
- *"It's not my job or duty to contribute."*
- *"Reward me just for being with you."*

Provision says,

- *"Our home and family deserves my proper care and consideration."*
- *"You can trust that the plans I have will be equally beneficial for us both."*
- *"I work to earn a living and to solidify and mobilize our plans for us."*
- *"My hard work is dedicated toward our future together."*
- *"I will offer security, comfort, and peace."*

Inferiority vs. Submission

Inferiority says,

- *"Whatever my partner says goes just because they said so. No questions asked."*
- *"My opinions and desires don't matter, but my partner's do."*
- *"I must tolerate disrespect, belittlement, humiliation, and mistreatment."*
- *"My thoughts and feelings are irrelevant."*

Submission says,

- *"I trust the plans you have for us."*
- *"You've proven that your leadership skills are worthy of my trust."*
- *"You've made me confident that you have our best interests at heart."*
- *"I trust that your maturity and sense of responsibility will lead us to success."*
- *"You give me peace and confidence to lean into you, your desires, and your suggestions."*
- *"Submission is for us both and is fluid within our relationship."*

Dictatorship vs. Partnership

Dictatorship says,

- *"Don't question me."*
- *"I don't owe you an explanation or have to prove myself to you."*
- *"I am in complete control."*
- *"If I go down, you're coming down with me."*
- *"I don't care to hear your input."*
- *"I must always have the final say."*
- *"If you don't do what I say and follow my lead, then there will be consequences."*

Partnership says,

- *"Let's come up with a solution together."*
- *"Sometimes we must each make sacrifices for the greater good of our relationship or personal betterment."*
- *"We discuss big plans first before making any final decisions."*
- *"Let's learn and grow together."*
- *"No matter if you fail or fly, I will support you. I am here for you."*
- *"We will lift each other up and get through our problems together."*

Knowing the true meanings of these terms, "submission" and "provision," could be the key to helping us break down any negative perception we've harbored in our hearts and minds over time. Believe it or not, having such a bitter outlook on what it means to be a provider or what it means to submit can be one of the main reasons why some members of our society—millennials especially—are having such a hard time finding and valuing true love.

I find it quite disheartening that, according to recent dating studies of 2020, 72 percent of millennials report that they've made a conscious decision to stay single.

Hmm, perhaps that's because 50 percent of the same participants also reported that they're concerned about engaging in long-term relationships.

As a member of the millennial generation, I must admit that I concur with most of the participants on both findings. Much like the women who were interviewed in the clinical study discussed earlier, I do have my doubts. But I refuse to allow my fears to hinder me from finding the relationship that God knows I deserve. My objective is to be a part of the solution—not just complain and contribute to the problem.

Chapter 4

Millennials' Pitiful Priorities: Birkin Bags and Game Systems

Recently, I was scrolling through my Instagram feed and noticed a trending topic among celebrities and my regular followers alike: #BirkinBag.

People—regular people with regular nine-to-five jobs—were in a frenzy about the expectation of their significant other gifting them a Birkin bag by Hermès.

Now, just in case you're wondering how much a Birkin bag costs or what the heck it even is, I'll be happy to tell you.

Hermès is a world-renowned, extremely high-end luxury goods maker. The family-owned French business began in 1837. Hermès prides itself on its sustainable yet artisanal contemporary style and its handmade items. Hermès has a plethora of opulent products that customers may purchase, including but not limited to the softest of silk scarves, genuine leather belts, jewelry, shoes, and fine fragrances.

Yet the most sought-after item created by Hermès is its ever so popular line of Birkin bags. Named after the model Jane Birkin, these handbags and purses are the epitome of immoderate extravagance. Birkin bags became especially popular within the African American community of entertainers, namely those within the music industry.

What makes them even more lust-worthy is how Birkins may also be customized or made-to-order originals.

This bag is not like any other bag you've heard of before.

I don't think you quite understand.

These bags are handcrafted and are available in various sizes. A customer can place a special order that details the specs of their one-of-a-kind bag. Artisans use authentic animal hide—anything from calf leather to lizard, ostrich, or even saltwater-crocodile hide—to fulfil the desires of their patrons. And you'd best believe that said patrons are ready and willing to pay top dollar for the best of the best.

Last time I checked (*only* to prove my point in this section of the book), the *least* expensive Birkin bag starts at twelve thousand dollars. However, with all the customizations—including hardware made using the most precious metals and even diamond-encrusted features—these bags can cost buyers half of a million dollars—and that's still on the "low-cost" end of the spectrum, believe it or not.

These highly coveted, incredibly rare handbags not only cost a pretty penny, but there's also a substantial wait list—with people who can potentially be waiting for *years* until their customized handbags are finally complete.

Do you get it now? These bags are incredibly hard to obtain and quite expensive, to put it lightly.

So why is it that millennials are the generation who cry the most about "the struggle" and how "broke" they are and how much living costs or how difficult "adulting" is, yet they expect lavish gifts from their partners as a means for them to prove how important they are to them?

Findings of the US Census Bureau (as of 2020) confirm that the average millennial makes less than 1,000 dollars per week, bringing the annual total for millennials to an estimated 47,043 dollars. Some may make more, and some may earn a little (or a lot) less.

However, there is no greater dissonance than what is between baby boomers and millennials (i.e., see #OKBoomer). Also, we can't forget the honorable mention goes to Gen Z. They shamelessly throw major shade at baby boomers as well.

But wouldn't people feel a little salty to know that while they love to talk trash about baby boomers, it's also been reported that millennials' average income is 20 percent less than what baby boomers earned when they were in the same age range as millennials (ages 24–39)? We may also consider that many millennials were growing up during the Great Recession, and that plays a large role in their incomes being substantially lower than some generations that had come before them.

It's true how young folks are quick to valiantly debate the unfairness of the generational wealth gap. They aren't afraid to publicly demand that the issue is not only acknowledged but also rectified. However, one thing that people are just gaining traction on—conversation-wise—is how the generational wealth gap worsens regarding African American millennials in particular.

That's why millennials, especially those who are Black, cannot afford to buy into the idea that provision begins and ends with gifts and financial sponsorship. They simply don't have the luxury to waste (yes, *waste*) money on expensive presents and outrageous vacations as tokens of their affection and appreciation.

Let me pause here to say that if you *are* an African American millennial who is way more well off (and I do mean *way more*), then spend away. Spend until your heart is content. If you invest more than you spend, you have multiple forms of income, your bills are paid on time (like clockwork), you are living without the help of parents or guardians, you are supporting yourself 100 percent, and you *still* have a substantial amount of surplus money at your own disposal, then you have my permission to completely disregard this section.

As for everyone else, kindly read on.

Here are just a couple of reasons why adopting outrageous spending habits in the name of "love" is hurting the relationships of Black millennials more than helping them:

The National Bureau of Economic Research published a series of working papers. NBER's May 2020 edition—*The Wealth of Generations, with Special Attention to the Millennials*—confirms that Black millennial households only make about 60 percent of what their white peers make.

Furthermore, a July 2020 article written by the *Business Insider* reports that Black millennials accumulate more student-loan debt, which leads to a greater struggle with finding a career post-graduation. Unfortunately, even when they do land careers, they earn less than their white counterparts—37,300 dollars annually compared to white young adults, who annually make 60,800 dollars on average.

This is not a reason to look at your white friends sideways the next time you see them. They've done nothing wrong to you by possibly making more money. It's just the way of the world and has been for quite some time.

Generally speaking, millennials of all races contribute to a brand of brilliance that they almost effortlessly exude. Thanks to consistent and rapid innovations in technology, newfound ways of earning an education from noteworthy and accredited institutes, and their not always "holy" boldness, they're put in much greater positions than generations before them. With the ever-growing access to resources and information, millennials are also more racially and ethnically diverse than previous generations.

Don't misunderstand me—the truth regarding the generational wealth gap is valid, and many of our money issues are out of our control. But at the same time, a lot of the additional financial problems that lots of millennials face stem from feeling the need to *look* like they're living their "best life" and give the impression that they've got it all together, yet they're more hesitant to put in the work to get it together *in real life*! Social media has, in a sense, made everything for show.

The point that I'm trying to make, ladies and gentlemen, is simple: going broke on gifts for your partner is not a form of provision. There. I said it.

And yes, I *will* say it louder for the people in the back.

Going broke on gifts for your partner is not a form of provision!

We are so busy trying to keep up with celebrities, we forget that we are comparing apples to oranges. Celebrities can afford their luxurious gifts and lifestyles. If we try to keep up with them, we end up skipping our car payments or being late on our mortgages. Trying to keep up with the gift-giving of celebrities is tarnishing our idea of provision.

And then there are women who honestly believe that if their man can't afford a designer bag for them, then they're not a good provider, and if their man isn't deemed as a good provider, they don't feel he's worthy of their submission—and the cycle continues.

I'd just like to say that I was tickled pink when I found out that so many regular people had so much to say about a topic they had no business weighing in on publicly. I wondered why people were so worried about getting a Birkin bag when that's not the tax bracket they're in.

In case you're confused, this is what I mean: Just because a certain amount of money is in your account doesn't mean it's *available* to you. I learned this the hard way myself—several times.

There is nothing wrong with wanting a life of luxury. There is nothing wrong with wanting nice, expensive things. But we get so caught up in *having* them, we forget we must *earn* them. We forget we must work our way to that level. We lust after things to the point that we'll jeopardize our financial well-being just to say we have this, or we own that.

Celebrities can comfortably afford it. It's pocket change to them. But a real provider is not going to allow their family's bank account to go in the negative so they can look good for people they don't know and sometimes don't even like. When celebrities are talking about gift-giving and "providing" and giving out so-called relationship advice, know who they're directing their message to before you take it personally. Ask yourself, "Is this any of my concern if they're discussing Birkin bags? Or am I not even rich enough to take their advice to heart because it has nothing to do with me?"

If Birkin bags weren't enough to throw social media into a tailspin, to get everyone all worked up again, the new PS5 game system just dropped this month too. The PS5 rivals the Xbox. Both are very pricey game systems that grown men spend a substantial amount of their leisure time playing, leaving wives and girlfriends to become anxious, petty, and passive-aggressive when the game systems get more of their attention than the women do.

Ironically enough, guys were jokingly (and some very seriously) declaring on social media how they expect to get the new PS5 from their partners as a gift.

Y'all, the controller alone can cost your so-called bae at least seventy dollars right off the bat. The entire PS5 game console starts at five hundred dollars.

Don't get me wrong, I love a good joke—more specifically a meme or viral social media post that hilariously illustrates the reality versus the expectation of the costly gifts that people have high hopes of receiving from their boos. It's just the susceptible individuals that I am truly worried about. Yeah, all of us can laugh and play about how your man better get you a designer handbag or how your woman better surprise you with a new game system for Christmas. But there are people who really believe in spending literally their last dime on things they simply do not need and God *knows* that they cannot comfortably afford.

Chapter 5

The Benefit of the Doubt

For a short period of time, I worked as a health concierge via a staffing agency. Employees from different companies would call us to get enrolled to their annual benefits program. My job was to troubleshoot any issues they were having while trying to go online and enroll on their own, or I'd just enroll them myself and answer any questions they had about their plans or the guidelines.

One day, a woman called, wanting to add her "domestic partner" to her benefits plan through her employer. The only problem was that her employer only allowed spouses to be covered under their health plan. If they weren't married, the only way someone could add their partner to their health plan was if their name had been on the lease or mortgage for the past twelve months in addition to a copy of an affidavit of marriage.

The woman stated her name and said, "I want to add my domestic partner to my benefits plan, but the forms of required documentation, I don't have."

I said, "Okay. Well, in order to prove that they're a domestic partner, you have to provide a copy of the lease with both your names on it. That's the company's way of proving that your domestic partner actually lives with you."

She quickly replied, "It's a mortgage. I don't lease. I own."

It's almost as if the sound of her own voice explaining to a perfect stranger her circumstances was making her self-conscious. (Sound familiar?) I couldn't help but notice that her voice went from a low, mumbling tone to a suddenly sassy and defensive one.

I said, "Okay, I'm sorry—a copy of the mortgage with your names on the document is required to add a domestic partner. That's what the term 'domestic' means."

Trying not to let her agitation get the best of her, she replied, "I know! His name isn't on the mortgage, but we've been living together for several months, so I just want to add him to my benefits plan."

I told her to at least start with obtaining an affidavit—a legal document that usually performs the same function as a marriage certificate but is used in place of one if the couple lost the original documentation. Affidavits are normally presented when applying for certain financial accounts or for insurance purposes.

I went on to explain what an affidavit was. She responded, clearly annoyed, "Okay, that's fine. I know what it is. Where and how do I get it?"

I was just as annoyed as her, but they paid me to keep my frustration under control no matter how irritating (or irritated) some callers could be.

I rolled my eyes; I was glad that she couldn't see me over the phone.

"Give me just a moment. I'm pulling it up on Google."

I—a twenty-five-year-old who never had a real boyfriend in her adult life, let alone a live-in romantic partner—had no idea how to obtain an affidavit either.

I don't know what the woman's situation was as to why she was in a domestic partnership with a man who, for some reason, had to be on her benefits plan through her employer in addition to his name not being on the "mortgage" despite the fact that they've been living together for "several months."

I gave them the benefit of the doubt. I thought it could be that he's physically unwell and she was acting as his caregiver. He could have recently become unemployed and hadn't been able to find work and couldn't afford his own home and was working toward getting back on his own feet and so on.

As my mind continued to wonder long after the call ended, I realized the possibilities were endless.

Dating and living with someone is cool, but that still doesn't have as many financial perks as getting married to that person.

Honestly, if you think about it, if you're with the one you absolutely love, marriage is just way more convenient.

It's like having VIP status throughout life with your significant other.

No, I'm not saying that people must jump into marriage after dating or living together for several months, but there are lots of advantages:

-Combined incomes could lead to a better mortgage rate

-More affordable rates on bundled home and auto insurance

-Health insurance for you both under the same plan can be obtained with ease

But that phone call from an annoyed woman did make me wonder.

Perhaps there's an underlying reason why a lot of folks simply don't want to get married—the fear of financial turmoil if they were to get a divorce.

I understand that not everyone is mushy like me. Not everyone dreams of that walk down the aisle to the altar, awaiting being legally tied to the person of their dreams forever and ever.

But this is what makes me a little sad: maybe we are more focused on how easy it would be to freely leave a domestic partnership than how easy it would be if we just got married (to the right person!) and worked everything out in order to not have to get a divorce in the first place.

Maybe ole girl was thinking, *Hey, sis, I know what I'm doing. If he acts up, I can kick his butt out and be well within my rights since his name isn't on the mortgage! And I'm gonna keep it that way!*

Okay, that's fine.

But I can't help but notice that it's almost as if our generation wants to do everything (literally *everything*) but get married.

They want to fall in love.

They want commitment.

They want to have babies.

They want to build wealth.

They want benefits in addition to *benefits*. (You get it.)

But why is it that someone can be doing all these things with the same person for years on end, but the possibility of marriage isn't even in the question?

It's almost as if we hope for the best but expect the worst (i.e., getting married and having all our money, time, and legal paperwork tied to someone just to inevitably have to fight our way out).

We board the relationship plane expecting things to eventually fall apart, so we abort and never make it to the ultimate destination: an everlasting love that forms a union honorable in the sight of God.

Chapter 6

Love Gets No Love

There's a love for money. There's a love for attention.

But the way millennials act, we prove that we do not have a love for love.

We quickly put on a pedestal and idealize what looks like "perfect" or "flawless" love. We have photos and #RelationshipGoals that circulate the internet, and we're fed this pristine picture of love, and we long for that picture-perfect, unrealistic love.

And we feel like if we can't have it that way, then there's no need for it at all.

If you have dreams, by all means, chase them. Work hard for what you want in life. You're not a heartless savage if you aggressively work to achieve your goals as an individual.

Whether we're single or in a relationship, I believe we can have whatever we work toward and whatever we value enough to put consistent effort into. But for lots of us, if we must choose between love or money, love or status, or love or recognition, most will choose the latter in every situation.

Putting money, status, or recognition before love could look like putting off a healthy relationship with a great person who shares your ambition, drive, and tenacity. But if things aren't financially or socially "perfect" for you and you haven't achieved your wildest dreams just yet, you discourage the idea of any kind of serious relationship with them.

I find it disheartening—the love we think we don't deserve because of the money and status we don't yet have.

Love sounds good to us, but when it comes down to it, our actions prove what we tend to prioritize and what we're willing to do without.

We prioritize money.

We're willing to do without love.

We are a selfish generation. Our generation seems to view love as merely a distraction and potentially a hindrance from achieving success. We value building for ourselves, not building with someone we love. The way we treat the people we love, it's as if money has an expiration date, or there's a cutoff time where you must make money, or it'll no longer be attainable for you. But it's actually the complete opposite.

Money doesn't have an expiration date.

The people you love, however, do.

Whether you lose them to death, they move on for themselves, or you lose them to another person, the one you love—the one whose precious presence you take for granted—won't always be there. Money will. But money can't bring back the person you love. Money can't console you or comfort you when you're missing someone who's out of your life forever.

What's worse is how we take for granted the time we have with those we love.

We'd rather spend our time working and racing the clock, trying to meet the deadlines we've inflicted upon ourselves and keep up with those we fear are more far ahead than we are. The time we could be spending with a significant other slips away while we're too busy thinking we have all the time in the world.

The fact of the matter is that we're wasting valuable time, worried about the wrong things and in a hurry to make and spend money that we can't take with us when our time is up.

And you never know when that could be, which is why it's important to cherish those we love while we can instead of pushing them aside or shutting them down until a "later time," which, frankly, isn't even promised to us.

Another quote I remember says, "There's only one thing more precious than our time, and that's who we spend it with."

Think back to January 26, 2020.

It was the day the entire world came to a stop after learning of the fatal helicopter crash that sadly claimed the lives of nine people—two of which were basketball legend Kobe Bryant and his thirteen-year-old daughter, Gigi.

Never in a million years could any of us have expected such a heart-wrenching tragedy, nor would we want to. Then I thought of Kobe's wife and mother of their four girls, Vanessa. My heart shattered for her.

Vanessa Bryant misses Kobe, her forever husband, and Gigi, her dear child, with her whole heart.

I pray their souls rest in eternal peace.

I'm sure Vanessa spent time with her family as often as their busy, sometimes-conflicting schedules allowed.

Yet, devastatingly so, Kobe and Gigi's departure was untimely.

Vanessa is incredibly wealthy.

But all the money in the world can't bring them back.

I saw a video clip of an interview that Kobe Bryant did, and it made my heart smile.

He was telling the story of when he and Vanessa met.

It's a little-known fact that before Kobe became a five-time NBA championship winner, he was an aspiring rap artist.

Vanessa, a high schooler at the time, was working as a model on the set of Kobe's video shoot.

Kobe talked about how sparks flew between him and her almost instantly on set.

After they exchanged numbers, he said they talked to each other for hours.

When Vanessa turned eighteen, she and Kobe were happily married.

Can you imagine if Kobe met Vanessa, the actual love of his life, and he pushed her away instead of giving in to what his heart was saying?

It would've been a shame if he told her, "I like you, but we shouldn't take each other seriously. I haven't made it big in the rap game yet. I'm not an NBA icon yet. I'm just a basketball rookie. You're not a world-renowned supermodel. You're still in high school, and you're just a video girl. Now's not the time for love. Instead, we need to focus on our financial and career aspirations as individuals."

But that's exactly what many people of our generation have done—push love away and chase after money and status.

Sometimes we sabotage God's plan because we think *we* have a better one.

Many of us have no idea how many of God's blessings we forfeited when we proved to him that we didn't deserve what he had in store for us.

During the interview, Kobe made a great point.

"When you're young, you really have the tendency to think about your own personal journey. For us, it was about taking two young people and trying to figure out our journey together."

Regardless of how young they were and what level of success they'd reached, Kobe and Vanessa *chose love* and let the rest happen according to God's plan.

And—wouldn't you know? —their love didn't take away from their success. As a matter of fact, their love *amplified* their success.

Their true love and commitment to each other is what led them to build an empire together and create a beautiful legacy.

We must stop putting money, titles, and status above the one and only thing that truly matters in the end: *love.*

Part 2

The Interviews

Over the course of three months, in between working a full-time job and still being mindful of other people's obligations and daily schedules, I conducted interviews. The questions I asked the subjects were all the same, and they were all in relation to the dynamics of provision, submission, and gender or relationship norms. Their responses gave me the most profound insights on all the different aspects that contribute to a person's decision to be single, date, be in a committed relationship, or get married.

The following conversations are unedited, and each subject made the conscious decision to verify their identity on a first-name basis.

These interviews quickly turned into passionate conversations, with dialogue that was transparent and organically fluid. As I spoke to each subject, I could tell how they yearned for this sort of conversation—whether they realized it or not. The opportunity to have an open, judgement-free discussion regarding the roles of men and women and reflect on their personal experiences and apply them to their current status was therapeutic; I've been dying to share the results.

(Single) Ladies First

Chapter 7

Aunyā: The Liberal Womanist

There's a phrase that goes something like this: "What's understood doesn't need to be said." However, your desires or expectations being left unspoken could lead to turmoil. As a matter of fact, I believe it's best *not* to go by this phrase, behaving as if your partner is a mind reader in terms of how you expect each other to conduct yourselves.

Yet, in life, while some rules are written, there are other rules that *are* unspoken. Anything prohibiting us from doing what we would ordinarily do, without any second thought, keeps us from reaping the potential consequences if these rules were broken.

So, there's no wonder why we don't really like to acknowledge (at least not out loud) how our partners may have certain rules they want us to abide by.

Meet Aunyā, 29—a self-proclaimed "liberal womanist." As a free-spirited, independent, and self-assured Black woman, she's no stranger to the dynamics of different relationships. While submission is traditionally the role of a woman, Aunyā sings my song of the fluidity of roles between man and woman.

"Some men will allow—quote on quote 'allow'—their partner or wife to go out. Some may not have a problem with them going out with their friends or going to clubs or bars. But there are those

who feel like, 'You are mine. What do you need to go out in that environment for and possibly entertain other men?'

So, then there's a situation where you have to decide whether you want to submit to that person and not go out to certain places. There are also women who don't want their men in that environment, and you have to make a decision. Do you submit to your partner?"

Think of the last time you were told what you were allowed and not allowed to do—probably when you were a child living under your parents' roof. Or perhaps you were given rules by your manager or an authoritative figure at work. In terms of monogamous relationships, for some, rules may just be in place as means of respect. Setting clear boundaries sounds better than setting "rules." But the fact of the matter is, submission goes hand in hand with *permission*.

"I think submission is a mutual thing. I don't think one partner should submit to the other based off a gender."

Just as well as submission is much more than saying yes, provision is more than giving your partner money or things. There are five love languages, but it seems like the one that's most important in this era is Giving and Receiving Gifts. There's also Physical Affection, Words of Affirmation, Acts of Service, and Quality Time.

Therefore, Aunyá feels that a man can have all the money in the world, but it still wouldn't matter if he can't love her the way she wants to be loved.

"We not only need finances, but we also need emotional support, physical support—we need all of that. He could have the money, but if he's not giving me what I really need within the relationship, I don't think I'd consider him a provider. You can give me all this money, but what if my love language is not Gifts? And mine isn't. My love languages are Quality Time and Physical Affection. I've been in relationships where my significant other was the 'provider' in the relationship, and I was not happy.

"There are a lot of things I can do [provide] on my own. My man being able to do it for me is just a plus. Don't get me wrong—the financial contribution is great because if we get married, that's a partnership. I don't have to worry—we're both bringing money to

the table. We both are able to contribute and provide. But there's more to it than finances."

So, of course, I had to ask the burning questions: "Would you say that it is pertinent that your man be the provider? How do you feel about earning more or less than him?"

"I'm dating to marry at this point. I don't have time to play. If we're bringing up submission and provision, if we can't contribute fifty-fifty, I need it to at least be sixty-forty, seventy-thirty—something. As long as we're both contributing financially.

"I can do bad all by myself. If I'm bringing 'the table,' you better slide your 'table' right next to mine! Ain't no 'You pull up a chair.' No, I need my man to bring another table. I can stay in my own place and have my own stuff, and I can be single and doing what I want to do.

"If we're talking about a partnership, we both have to be contributing. If one of us is making less, we'll have to be on a budget so that we're good. I'm not a stickler as far as the dollar amount. I just need someone who's going to be motivated, and if it comes down to it, we got it.

"I don't mind making more as long as it's not a significant amount. I don't want either one of us feeling overwhelmed or going broke trying to handle everything alone."

Aunyā's belief of the roles being fluid between man and woman is part of the reason why she prides herself on being a liberal womanist.

"That's just my personal view. I have friends who have those traditional roles, and I am all for it. I empower them to live their life how they wanna live it. I'm here for whatever you wanna do. I have my own personal beliefs, but that doesn't make me look at you any differently."

Aunyā is admittedly nontraditional herself, but she also believes in the peace and power of women doing what they feel comfortable doing within relationships.

"If you're someone who wants to follow traditional roles, that's your prerogative. I'm not gonna judge you or your relationship if

that's what y'all wanna do. If you're okay with it and so is your partner, it's none of my business."

Now, to be clear, just like any other alpha woman, Aunyā is not afraid to take the lead if necessary. However, within a monogamous relationship, she's open to yielding to a man who's proven his leadership skills in a logical and respectful manner.

"I think it takes a level of trust. Trusting that whoever you are submitting to that they're wise about the decisions they make or their actions. I have a very dominant personality, but I will be submissive if I feel like I can trust that person's judgment."

Trust can truly make or break a relationship. Aunyā was my first interview subject (or my "guinea pig," as I jokingly referred to her as). Unbeknownst to us, she started the common idea among my remaining interview subjects of how trust is essentially the key that opens the door to submission.

It kind of makes me think of that one team-building or trust-building activity. You know the one I'm talking about? One person stands behind another. Then, the person standing at the front with their back facing the other closes their eyes and falls backward, trusting that the individual behind them will catch them in their arms.

I'm sure y'all have seen this before.

Well, that's what submission is like in a way. You put your faith in your partner and their plans, believing that they won't let you fall. Of course, you know that they should be able to trust that you won't let them fall either. When it's their turn to believe in or submit to you when you say, "You can fall back. I've got you," they can trust that you really mean it.

Still, being a preacher's kid, Aunyā made it clear that whoever's "got her" must be a man of God.

"With me having a relationship with God, being a Christian, if my man is asking me to do something and I'm like 'I don't think that's something God would want me to do,' then I won't do it."

She made a simple yet valid point. Submitting to your partner, whether you're the man or the woman, should never make you go against your morals or your faith. Submission and provision are both much easier when you share the same values and have respect for each other's beliefs.

"I think that's why it's very important that you're equally yoked with your partner because you are pretty much gonna be on the same page. Your thinking is the same. You have some of the same goals, so it's a little bit easier to submit to your partner. It doesn't feel like such a strain."

Recently, I said it seems as though our generation doesn't value marriage. It could be that most are just reluctant due to the risks of marriage. And I credit this to, once again, the negativity surrounding gender roles or our lack of desire to submit or provide. If nothing else, we are not placing as much of an emphasis on marriage as generations before us.

In terms of being equally yoked, there are couples who feel the same about getting married. While some make it clear in the dating stage that they share the same ultimate goal, which is to be wed after a certain amount of time, there are others who are more laid-back and feel as though love and the legitimacy of a partnership don't need to be solidified by marriage, which is only "man-made" or "just a piece of paper."

As I said earlier, I get that it's not everyone's fantasy to make it down the aisle. But that can become a major issue if expectations are unclear or if you've been inadvertently following the "what's understood doesn't need to be said" phrase. It sort of goes back to Aunyā's point about the importance of being equally yoked. When you fail to see eye to eye on the most concrete principles, there's bound to

be a downward spiral.

When it comes to expectations while dating and behavioral patterns formed early on, Aunyā calls it the way she sees it.

"They can do all that you want them to do up front. But if they're actually not ready to be that person that you need, that inconsistency is going to be there. You can't fake stuff for too long. You can't maintain the facade.

Guys, nine times out of ten, know exactly what kind of woman they're working with. They know what you're worth even before you know what you're worth as a woman. With that, they know what they can do and what they can't do."

In other words, stating what you desire, what you need, and what you expect comes first. Submission and provision will flow naturally afterward. After all, you can't provide something to someone if they're not even sure of what they want for themselves, let alone for the both of you. On the other hand, you can't submit to someone when you have no idea of their true motives or their ultimate intentions.

Chapter 8

Katrina: The Straight Shooter

"Slave. A man's slave. You are his property. You are his slave. You are just gonna do what you're told to do. When I think of submissive, I think of **Coming to America.** *The young lady that was barking in the gold dress? That, to me, is a version of submission."*

Well, folks, meet Katrina, 39.

When asked the question "What is your definition of 'submission'?" her response made me laugh. She's got a brand of humor that is dry and sarcastic yet blunt and matter-of-fact. It's no wonder that one of her favorite movies is the Eddie Murphy classic *Coming to America*. If you haven't seen this before, *shame on you!*

Just kidding. But seriously, you should watch it.

Prince Akeem, Murphy's character, has come of age and is to be married to his country's, Zamunda's, most beautiful eligible woman, Imani Izzi. She was handpicked at birth by Prince Akeem's royal parents.

Now first, let's get into the song "She's Your Queen," which is sung by one of the castle men as Imani Izzi made her way to Prince Akeem. With lines like "A queen who'll do whatever His Highness desires" and "To be used at your discretion, waiting only for your direction," it's unbelievable how many times I watched this movie myself and I never tripped off the lyrics! The blatant declaration of how his wife would be extremely subservient in such an inferior way was laughable once I finally tuned in.

The queen-to-be was in pristine condition. She was covered from head to toe in shimmering golden jewels—just glistening in sparkling splendor. Prince Akeem requested that she tell him more about herself and tried to find some form of individuality within the queen-to-be but soon realized that she was not interested in anything but following his orders. As a matter of fact, her exact words were "Ever since I was born, I've been trained to serve you."

Imani Izzi's submission to Prince Akeem was inhumane—almost robotic even. Just to test her, Prince Akeem asked her, "Are you saying that no matter what I tell you to do, you will do? Anything I say, you will do?"

Imani Izzi smiled and bowed her head with grace and responded, "Yes, Your Highness."

Suddenly, Prince Akeem commanded her to bark like a dog while hopping on one leg and then grunt like an orangutan.

You better believe that the queen-to-be did just that without question.

Completely turned off by Imani's inability to have a mind of her own and her lack of respect for herself, Prince Akeem goes to America on a quest to find the woman of his dreams. He wanted not just a woman who was graceful and beautiful but a woman who would have backbone and take more pride in thinking and speaking for herself—a woman with dignity and intellect. He vowed to find that kind of woman in America and bring her to his home country so they could be wed and live happily ever after.

When Katrina initially answered my first question, I couldn't help but laugh. But even though I was laughing, I also couldn't help but notice the key word she used toward the end of her response; she said that was a *"version"* of submission. That proved to me that she was aware that there are variations of submission. Yes, some are quite extreme or even hysterical—just like the queen-to-be who barked like a dog at her prince's command.

Katrina admittedly referred to women being submissive as slavery, then moments later, she still made it clear that men should provide and oversee the household. Ironic, right? Just hear her out.

"I agree that men should be the provider. I firmly believe that men should be the head of the household. A man should lead you in the direction that you should be—the number one goal is closer to God—and then lead you elsewhere. He's the strength of the household, and the woman is to help carry the household, but the man is supposed to be the lead."

Although this is Katrina's prototype of a real man, she expressed why she has reservations regarding the men of this generation and how there's a clear divide between the older gentlemen and the younger ones, more specifically millennials.

"To me, there's like a divide. So, what I mean by that is, the older generation—and when I say 'older,' I mean age fifty and up—I've noticed they have more of an understanding of what marriage should be and what a man is supposed to provide within a marriage."

"The younger generation, in my opinion, has lost all understanding of that. The younger generation tends to demoralize men in terms of relationships. It's almost as if people are jumping into relationships not understanding what the man's responsibility is, what his goal is, or even what the end goal is."

Katrina went on to express how the younger generation has tainted the way she views and how our contemporary culture views young Black men as providers.

"There's a loss that's there, and to me, it makes the younger generation look weak, not like providers. But at the same time, I've noticed that some younger men have allowed that [demoralization, "weak" narrative] to further perpetuate because that foundation [the teachings or upbringing of a positive male role model or father figure] doesn't seem to be there.

"I often see the difference between my dad and my uncles versus my nephews. My parents and my uncles are in their sixties and

seventies. The mentality is different. You don't see young men even wanting to be providers.

"They're so comfortable staying with their moms in basements, not working, the girlfriend's working, and taking care of the kids, while some of them are just out running the street. That mental grounding, as far as what a man is supposed to be, it's not there in the younger generation."

One word: *Ouch.*

Perception is reality, and everyone is entitled to their own perception as well as their own opinion. Again, no one came to condemn or shame, but I did encourage everyone to freely and honestly speak *their* truth. During our interview, however, Katrina, the youngest of six, did admit that her upbringing and what she witnessed throughout her childhood are what shaped her personal standpoint regarding provision and submission.

"I saw a lot of stuff growing up. My upbringing was rough. I use the phrase jokingly, but I'm still very serious when I say [my parents' relationship] was very The Color Purple-ish. *My parents are straight from the South, so they had a very southern upbringing. There was a lack of education, and they were very submissive at an early age just to get out of certain situations.*

"What I mean by that is, my parents were cotton pickers. So, their way out of that situation was to marry and move away. They married young [seventeen and eighteen years old]. They had no education—no knowledge. Men worked. Women bore children."

The Color Purple is another star-studded classic, with Whoopi Goldberg, Danny Glover, and Oprah Winfrey. This award-winning coming-of-age historical drama is especially popular among the African American community. *The Color Purple* tells the harrowing story of a young Black girl in the South during the age of slavery and the civil rights movement who was married off by her father to a belligerent and demeaning man more than twice her age.

Forced into womanhood, bearing children, and tending to the needs and commands of her much older husband, she was left with no choice but to fend for herself and to navigate the woes of abuse and, more than anything, severe bigotry and sexism.

As Katrina said, marrying at a young age, just as her parents did, was the only thing young African Americans could do as a means of survival and to get ahead in life. Forming a legal union enabled them to earn more money collectively and conceive children who would soon be able to work and carry on the family name, which could bring a greater chance of wealth and stability into the family's lineage; these were the goals of many Blacks brought up especially during the 1930s up to the 1950s.

"There was that line of submission that was there for even me growing up, and I'm an eighties baby. I came along around the time when my mom chose to learn how to do stuff herself instead of relying on my dad. It was decades later, and my mom was learning to drive, trying to enter the workforce, and she was in her late thirties or early forties at this point. She spent so much time just being what my dad wanted.

"My father was never at home and always worked. My mom was the provider and caretaker for the kids, but at the same time, she was that submissive one in the household.

"It wasn't necessarily 'Do as I say' type of submissive. She made sure he had food on the table every single day—breakfast, lunch, dinner—made sure his clothes were ironed, made sure he didn't have a reason to fuss about anything, made sure he was attended to—but in my opinion, she was attending to too much, and so it became demoralizing.

"Once it got to the point where she stepped into her own, it was like the clash of the titans occurred. Now he can't control what she's doing, where she's going, or who she's with. Now, his chicken wasn't on the table at five o'clock, like it typically was."

Because of what she witnessed while growing up, Katrina knew that she wanted better for herself, relationship-wise.

"There was one guy I dated as an adult, and he believed in that 'submissiveness.' He wanted a woman who didn't work and stayed at home. This is a guy that I actually liked, but once he mentioned

that, I was like, 'You're not even a candidate for me anymore.' I'm going to work. I'm going to earn my own income. That was one thing my dad held over my mom's head—money. It was like he put her on an allowance. Ain't no way I'm gonna let a man do that to me.

"If there are certain things that a guy says to me that even seem 'submissive,' I'm going to cut him short. I've seen other couples who do it effectively. But my parents didn't have a partnership."

This is what life is all about, right? We grow, we observe, and we learn—not just from our own mistakes but from other people's mistakes as well. Still, it is just as important not to allow the traumas of your past and any negative influences you've been subjected to, to cause discord in your own relationships.

It may be hard to accept it, but just as I stated earlier, our gender schemas and the expectations that we were taught or what we witnessed play a huge role in our perception of others and certain situations that we find ourselves in.

Katrina mentioned how she had to take a step back and analyze her decision-making process when choosing a potential mate.

"I have to catch myself in regard to not cutting people off so quickly just because of my background. Now, I'm more open to talking about it and trying to figure out how I can overcome some of these issues. There are some men who want to be providers—not a woman to just do everything they say. They simply just want to be providers. But I had to learn how to back off and understand that there's a difference."

Here's the thing: When Katrina first answered my original question, she wasn't referring to the true definition of "submission." Remember the "Misunderstanding vs. Reality" chapter? Yeah, I think it's quite evident that Katrina was speaking from the standpoint of misunderstanding, which is the complete opposite of healthy submission; it is, in fact, inferiority (i.e., *"I must tolerate disrespect, belittlement, humiliation, and/ or mistreatment,"* *"Whatever my partner says goes just because they said so. No questions asked,"* etc.).

Don't be fooled. First of all, if your partner genuinely loves you, they will never make you feel inferior to them. Even the Bible says that love is not proud and does not dishonor others (1 Cor. 13:4–8). That means that you should not treat them in a condescending manner or place yourself above them, nor should you think more highly of yourself than you think of your partner. Therefore, if your partner, man or woman, evokes any feelings of inferiority within you, then it is time for you to completely move on from them—like, for real.

Chapter 9

Cynthia: The Mogul in the Making

A woman of many hats, especially if that woman is Black, must almost effortlessly balance a tremendous amount of responsibility with the utmost grace and finesse. Well, that brings us to my next interview subject. Cynthia is the epitome of "thirty and flirty and thriving." If you know, you know.

Okay, okay! I'll tell you.

In the blockbuster *13 Going on 30,* Jennifer Garner's character was all of us when we were young, awkward adolescents. Juggling high school, secret crushes, and mean girls, the quirky thirteen-year-old main character was just desperate to fast-forward her life and instantly become the beautiful, sexy, and successful woman of her dreams.

Cynthia, 30, became certified in a popular cosmetology trade and started an LLC, making her the CEO of her company. In addition to running her successful business, she is also a full-time employee holding a key position at a Fortune 500 conglomerate, the creator and cohost of an up-and-coming podcast, *and* a chairwoman and big sister of a mentorship program that serves underprivileged, well-deserving young girls.

As a natural-born hustler, provision isn't necessarily something that a woman like Cynthia will sit around and wait for from a man, a friend, or anyone else, for that matter. If someone is used to moving the way

51

they want and calling their own shots every day, it might feel a bit unorthodox for them to tap into a more submissive side—and it can be even more challenging depending on whether they've ever witnessed any form of submission while growing up.

"I think that it's definitely more difficult for a Black woman to do because there's been so many generations of single-parent households where women have had to raise and take care of entire families by themselves. A lot of young ladies come from a family of women that have raised kids on their own, and some of them have that 'We don't need a man' mentality."

I couldn't have agreed with her more. I too have witnessed strong Black women do it all on their own and quite well—everything from raising their children to earning an honest living and providing their kids' needs as well as many of their desires. These women have sacrificed much of their own lives and put the needs of their children before themselves without the leadership or sometimes even the *presence* of a man.

"It's difficult if you've never seen your mother submit to a man. You haven't seen these 'strong' women around you submit to a man. They've been doing things on their own. I don't even think some women know what submission looks like anymore—outside of their grandparents or their great-grandparents. I don't think we even have the tools or the resources to understand what submission is."

Our first teachers are our parents or our parental figures. What we observe at a young age sets the tone for how we will behave or what our expectations are as adults—once again, they're the first contributors to our gender schemas. The examples that our parents exhibited are often what we mimic when we come of age.

For instance, submission may come easier for a woman who's witnessed this role or behavior in its healthiest form. If she hasn't been misled into believing that submission is for the weak or that it means that she must tolerate mistreatment, she'll more than likely have no problem with developing a relationship and submitting to a man who has proven his capability for provision.

Nevertheless, there's a bit of a difference between women who submit today and women who submitted fifty years ago. Women back in the day submitted mainly out of obligation or customary practices. Submitting to their man was something they *just did*. It's just the way things went in a heavily patriarchal generation. Now, in 2021, the inclinations and the intellect of women have evolved.

"Every conversation we have about submission and provision on social media has just been a back-and-forth about traditional versus modern mentality. Submission used to be because 'My man is the leader of this household. He pays all the bills, and he's the breadwinner.' I think the intent behind submission has changed.

"I think women used to submit back in the day so easily because their man was the sole provider, and it was almost like you could lose your sense of stability in the event that you went against your man. You were basically risking it all. Your family was going to be broken, you wouldn't have had a home, you couldn't pay the bills [back when women didn't even work].

"Now the intent behind submission is almost like a conservative or a traditional thought. I think the modern-day woman is completely different than the woman back in the day that used to submit. Now, women have multiple streams of income, so they don't have to depend on a man."

Reflecting on Cynthia's striking points, it begs these inquiries: Are there still some women today who only submit because they feel like they have to? Is submission, in some cases, contingent upon whether women are dependent upon their men financially or socially? Are women who are more independent and financially stable *less* likely to be submissive? Should your independence have anything to do with your willingness to be led by your man?

With all these factors coming into play, it could further muddy the waters.

"It's very difficult in our culture today to be submissive to a man because it's almost like viewed as a weakness because Black women have had to be so strong and they've had to do so much independently, and they've been self-sufficient for a while now."

I was born during the girl-group era. I loved me some 3LW, TLC, and SWV when I got a little older. But Destiny's Child *insert dramatic pause here* was and still is my all-time favorite. When I was about six years old, Destiny's Child released one of their greatest hits to date, "Independent Women Part I." I vividly remember my mom blasting this song in the car while cruising down the highway, singing with such passion, sass, and confidence that it literally gave me goose bumps.

Something about this song felt so empowering—even at the age of six! Mind you, this was a song that I wouldn't be able to relate to for *years* to come. Still, it moved me in a way that I couldn't even begin to define.

So, I get it. Self-sufficiency brings a feeling of power, and we take pride in being able to do things on our own. Being a self-made woman and getting your success "out the mud" feels much better than someone being able to say, "You wouldn't have that if it weren't for me." Plus, we live in a time when everything is broadcast on social media. It's become a place where people seek advice and where they dissect their innermost thoughts and values.

That's why it's important to keep certain things off social media and find a genuine friend or a professional counselor to talk to in private and with confidence—but I digress. What I'm trying to say is, if we aren't careful with where we find solace and seek validation, the response can be more harmful than helpful.

There are some women who struggle with how others view them depending on their decision to be submissive to a man. While some women may take more of a neutral stance to "live and let live," there are others who publicly pity the woman who yields to her man.

"Honestly, I've seen women [on social media] be open about submitting to their man, and I'll look in the comments, and other women are responding negatively—as if 'submit' is a bad word. Telling the world that your man is good enough to submit to, because it's seen as such a bad thing, the average woman is looking like 'Humph, that's you, not me.'

"Especially women who are not in relationships or those who haven't been in the best of relationships, they're looking at you like

'I mean, if that's what you wanna do, that's cool, but that's not cute.'
Submission is just not seen as a good thing—almost like they think
it means you just let your man do whatever to you, but that's not
what submission really is in my opinion."

According to Cynthia, submission is more about making the conscious decision to be led in order to show your man that you trust him and respect his role as the man and all that it encompasses.

"Submitting in marriage, from a woman's standpoint, is
allowing your mate to lead you. I think, for most men to feel like
they are the head of the household or in order to feel like the man
in the relationship, they need some level of submission. Of course, I
also think there needs to be room for compromise."

Very well said. I believe that compromise is a pertinent component of any solid partnership. When one partner is digging their heels in the dirt, it's going to be tough to gain submission from being stubborn. In turn, being a provider is a way to portray the authentic traits of a real *leader*—compassion and leniency, but they must also bring the best out of their partner.

You show your plants love by giving them plenty of water and sunlight. You show your car love by getting an oil change on schedule and keeping it clean. So obviously, your partner has needs and special ways they must be cared for as well.

"When I think of provider, I think of them being the breadwinner
or whatever. But for me personally, it's providing me the things that
I need in my love language. Outside of my love language, being able
to provide me with a sense of security. I'm just recently starting to
date again. The person I am exclusively dating now is really big on
my love languages—Physical Touch and Words of Affirmation.

"A lot of my previous relationships had been practical. So I
could see a man being a provider, I could see myself being in a stable
relationship with them and they weren't going to cheat, but they
weren't big on my love languages. Me not requiring it or expecting
it didn't help. But now that I'm being loved in my love language, I
see how important it is."

So, just like Aunyā, Cynthia sees provision as so much more than showering a woman in material things and showing a woman what he can do for her or what he can buy for her. Yet what we consume from the media is damaging some people's outlook on provision.

"I feel that we live in a very savage culture. These girls are requiring men to buy them Louis, Gucci, Prada bags in order to feel like the man is worth their time, energy, and effort. That's because of this current hip-hop culture and social media and celebrities and seeing how their relationships are.

"'Provider,' for this culture that we're in, means the expectation is for a Black man to come into the relationship, pay your bills, and buy you bags. That's what people think a provider is."

We can be real! Who *wouldn't* be the least bit impressed if their partner were to do these things—if they were financially able? It's not a bad thing to spoil your partner. It's not a bad thing if you are like many of us who enjoy *being* spoiled. What *is* a bad thing is setting these unrealistic expectations for your partner, especially someone you *just met* or someone you just became serious with.

Love and loyalty should never be measured by how many gifts you receive or how quick they are to pay your rent. We must allow love to be love—not a meal ticket.

Eligible Bachelors

Chapter 10

Daryel: The Cool, Calm, and Collected

Inquisitive. Meditative. Relaxed. Just a few words to describe Daryel, 27.

He was the first single man to participate and be interviewed for this project, and when I asked if he was interested, his response was a resounding "Yes!"

Now, finding single Black women who were excited about participating and being interviewed was a breeze. On the other hand, coming across single Black *men* who were just as delighted to discuss gender roles, provision, and submission was like finding needles in a haystack. So you can imagine how relieved I was when he said he was "ecstatic" to have such an important conversation with me.

Oh, and real quick, I'll let y'all in on a little secret: To all of you men out there who are afraid of sharing your innermost thoughts or showing any ounce of vulnerability, thinking it makes you seem too "soft" or undesirable to women, let me just say, you couldn't be more wrong.

A man being secure enough in his masculinity to be respectfully honest and open about how he feels is—I cannot stress this enough—the *ultimate* turn-on for us women.

Just a little food for thought.

Anyway, what do you get when a man is quite articulate about his needs and beliefs, plus he's aware of the misconceptions circulating within our society? You get this guy.

While some may be a little more tainted based off what they saw while growing up, others choose to take those experiences and use them to evolve and become more thoughtful and open-minded when faced with similar issues.

Daryel reflected on his childhood and what he witnessed between his parents.

"My mom and my ole dude had me at a pretty young age. It was their first lil' finagle, I guess. I didn't grow up in a home with married parents. I grew up in a traditional single-parent home. Honestly, since I'm an observant person, it made me pay attention to what was there and what was missing—not for me but between my parents."

Exactly. Where misunderstanding is paired with the usual growing pains of two young adults who are coparenting, naturally, there could be some conflict along the way. But witnessing conflict between those we love allows us to form an objective opinion, having seen and heard both sides of the story from the outside, looking in.

Still, our perspective is from the *outside*. So our point of view and what we choose to do with what little we actually *can* see and comprehend are crucial.

"Like I said, they were young, so I watched them go through the stages in life while they were growing mentally and spiritually. They had some growing challenges that I was a part of. I wasn't looking at it in a negative way, though. I saw how they responded to each other, trying to open their minds and understand each other. Watching them helped me put things into perspective as far as how I would become or who I wanted to be as a father, maybe a husband."

At that moment, I felt Daryel may have indirectly confirmed his desire to become a father or a husband in the future. He later expounded on his previous comments.

"It's crazy how I said it in that order—father then a husband. A lot of times, people, including me, are comfortable with having a baby, but when it comes to fully committing to a person—in a marriage—it requires even more of a commitment and dedication. That's how things are. I even had a conversation with someone, and

I told them if I find somebody I'm cool with, that I can trust that they ain't gonna fuck me over, then I'll just have a kid with that person."

There you go. His point is contrary to the cynical narrative that's perpetuated, which says that there are "no more good men" and how "men only want one thing."

Some Black men's problem is meeting a decent woman with whom they feel comfortable building these bonds of partnership and parenthood. *That* is what Daryel feels may be a little more elusive.

"As a man, you're looking for your 'other half.' But some women out there are just looking for the money. They're not looking for morals and other things like that."

For Daryel, although he revealed his reservations, he feels it's important for a Black man to find true love. Daryel also believes that the key to a Black man finding true love is finding a Black woman who'll just be his serenity. A woman that a man can count on to be his oasis away from life's many attacks and troubles is what most decent Black men truly long for.

Instead, many are met with someone who brazenly has their hand out, applying an obscene amount of pressure for him to reward her with a life of luxury in addition to successfully manning the ship that is the family household *and* directing them to financial stability and spiritual comfort.

Black women and Black men have made great strides in the world and are steadily breaking barriers and reaching new heights. However, Black men specifically still face their fair share of adversity and must work twice as hard as their White counterparts. Daryel suggested that this can be concerning for some Black men if they're not quite in the position to "provide" the lifestyle a woman desires. Still, that doesn't mean that those men can't provide in other ways.

"Not every Black man is put in that position to win. Because of the way society is set up, as we can all see, there's a lot of adversity we face. Whether it's growing up in a neighborhood where you're in a consistent battle of trying to be better than the next person and trying to elevate to either being targeted or overlooked by the authorities or people who are put in the position to protect you.

"Black men face challenges constantly, and they don't really have too much of an outlet or that peace they expect to come from their woman. Black men have so much against them as it is, then to meet a woman who's immediately like 'I need you to do this, this, and that' adds to that tension. Some men are still growing.

"That's not to say that men should be dependent on anyone for their growth. I just feel that not every man is in that position to 'provide' in that way right off the bat."

"A lot of women focus on more of a specific way of providing. I think the term 'provider' is a lot broader than what people realize. It's more than just on the financial tip. I feel like you can provide in whatever way possible, but I also feel like it depends on the people who are involved in that marriage."

To piggyback off Daryel's point, I have to interject here and say that *this is exactly why* it is so important to learn and understand your partner way before marriage is considered. Everyone's needs and wants are different. Speak to your partner. Develop healthy ways, even if they're nonconventional, to communicate.

If you don't get anything else from this entire book, I want you to know it is one of my main goals that we let go of the fear and anxiety that are sometimes attached to *communication*. Just a simple, respectful briefing could prevent a plethora of petty quarrels.

"You go through phases in life where you feel like you're with the right person. Next thing you know, you hate that MF. It's the truth! With that being said, in the beginning stages of a relationship, as far as provision and submission, I don't owe you anything, and you don't owe me anything. I'm just asking that you show me who you are.

"Allow me to learn and love who you are. Let me learn your core values. Let me see if I can align with you, and we can go from there. If it doesn't work out, so be it.

"You don't say "til death do us part' as boyfriend and girlfriend. We can be boyfriend and girlfriend in the morning and exes by two o'clock. Just that quick—like 'This ain't working out.'"

Daryel says that submission is also about adaptation. Any woman who is sharp-witted and proactive enough to take complete charge of her own business or entrepreneurial endeavors and make tough decisions every day can surely use a break every now and again. If she trusts her man, you better believe that it may just be something she can get used to, allowing him to take the reins every now and then—not necessarily taking orders or being undermined by him but instead being shown that there's someone who can take charge to ease her mind.

"With life, I feel like everybody can adapt in some form or fashion. But people get used to being on their own. When they're faced with something new [like having to adapt within a relationship], they have to conform. They begin to compromise and make things work. I'm not in that position, but I'm sure love will make you submit to certain things you normally wouldn't."

Regardless of whether you're a man or a woman, most of us don't take too kindly to demands or inconsideration. Wouldn't you agree? No man wants a woman who has a laundry list of baecation expectations and Chanel bags that she is waiting for him to provide. Conversely, when it comes to submission, "Sit down, be quiet, look pretty, and just do as I say" isn't quite Daryel's style when he is dating a woman on a monogamous level.

Daryel is proof that you can be a strong, masculine "man's man" and still take heed of your woman when it's necessary. When a man is mature and possesses confidence and humility, he won't be the least bit taken aback or intimidated by a woman who is intentional and holds her own.

Just like there are men out there who are used to always, always, *always* being in control, and it's hard for them to imagine the thought of relinquishing that leverage, it's also true that some women aren't used to being led; *they're always the leaders.*

I know, right? Mind. Blown.

(I hope you know that I said that with the utmost sarcasm.)

"I feel like, as a man, you can be the leader and the head of the household, but then there's a time when you have to step back. You have to submit. Y'all have to come to an agreement. You can't run everything.

"Whenever I do settle down, I would want a woman with alpha tendencies. That would make me feel more upscale, if I have a woman who was dominant with other men but she decided to submit to me. If that's the case, my woman just boosted me up. If she's just submitting to anyone because she likes his style or whatever, she sounds a lil' goofy to me."

So there you have it. There is so much more to a relationship than showing how agreeable you can be. The strength of a true partnership has never been about surrendering your power or being programmed to automatically placating your partner in every situation.

Contrary to what some people believe, a healthy relationship is more about recognizing the importance of your voice alone and realizing the power of both voices when they're in accord.

Chapter 11

Odjo: The Southern Gentleman

Before the start of every interview, I read off a list of disclaimers to my subjects. During the reading of the disclaimers, everyone was informed of their choice to either keep their identity confidential or grant me the permission to refer to them on a first-name basis.

Odjo, 25, proudly stated, "Use my name!"

And it was at that moment that I knew . . .

This man must know he's about to drop some gems.

At just five years old, Odjo traveled all the way here from the Ivory Coast, his father's country of origin. His mother is a native of Haiti.

Although extenuating circumstances delayed his father from initially relocating along with them, Odjo, his brother, and their mother came to the States and made a life for themselves in Florida. Soon after, Odjo's father arrived in Florida as well, happily uniting their family once again.

Born in Africa and raised there until his family's departure, Odjo was transported to a Western society that truly was a whole new world. He credits his African-Haitian upbringing for his constructive perspective of provision and submission.

"We don't consider how people are raised. I think that has a lot to do with how you view provision, how you view yourself as a man, how you view yourself as a husband. My parents are both non-Western. My mom is Haitian, and my dad is African. I was

born in Africa. So, their cultural norms are a little bit different. As a provider, I think American terms are different than in other countries."

Good point. Of course, everyone's upbringing may compare and contrast in many ways. More specifically though, Odjo refers to the ever-so-eclectic experience of each Black person as an individual, thus causing us to all have different outlooks, which leads to us living out different truths—regardless of if they're "wrong" or "right."

"I feel like the collective Black experience is so unique. You don't know what kind of environment they had growing up. You don't know how people saw their parents. I consider myself fortunate to grow up in the household I did. I know not everyone had the same luxury [of two loving parents]. I understand that shapes people's perception of relationships and gender norms."

Odjo gave me insight on where his morals and values are derived, attributing his outlook on the correct dynamics of provision and submission to what he witnessed between his two devoted parents.

"With my parents, both not being as American or as Western as most people here, I feel like the lifestyle they embodied completely changed the way I viewed relationships and the way I viewed women. That's important, especially as a Black man. Our biggest examples are within our household, and we all know the stereotypes regarding absent fathers and things like that.

"My mom, my brother, and I came to America sooner than my dad. But when my dad came here to the States, no one would recognize his teaching certificate. So, for the longest—I'm talking a year and a half, two years—he could not find work. So, my mom was the breadwinner in our household."

At this point, Odjo referenced one of the many infamous memes or social media posts that spoke on the preference of the man paying all the bills within a relationship.

For the record, I can proudly and honestly say that any negative social media posts referenced throughout this book *do not* reflect the views of myself or any of my interview subjects.

Odjo says his role and duties as a provider will be dependent upon what his woman's needs are and what she's communicated to him, and he'll take pride in his capability to oblige her in those areas.

"Being a provider is more than just finances, but that's what we always dwindle it down to. For example, who's supposed to be paying the bills? As a matter of fact, I've seen the social media posts and people making jokes like, 'If I want a roommate, then I'll just get a roommate. I'm not splitting bills with my man.' I'm sure, as the man, when he couldn't find work, my dad's pride was hurting a little bit or whatever.

"But I think the one thing my mom did was a good job at holding him up. That's so big for a couple, especially for an African American couple. There was never any pressure. There were never any feelings of discontent or my mom making him think he wasn't man enough because he couldn't provide.

"They still handled everything together. It was a joint effort. They made sure we were straight and put their own needs last. Even when my mom found work as a guidance counselor and as a teacher, whenever my father found work, he didn't have any luxurious jobs or anything like that. He literally worked to make ends meet. My mom used the car. My dad took a bike to work."

That's dedication. That's devotion—not just devotion to each other as husband and wife, but they were also devoted to the greater good of the family—more than anything else. There was no power struggle; rather, there was a keen sense of responsibility and humility.

When Odjo spoke to me about his parents and their partnership, I was inspired by their tenacity and grit. The way they strategically made a commitment to relocate to America and made strides to reach their goals as a unit, they gave me strong 'by any means necessary' vibes.

"It wasn't even about submission. It was just doing what you have to do as a couple. I think that's what really shaped my perspective. It's not really important who has the 'power' in the relationship. Of course, when my dad started making more money, it was a lot easier, and we were struggling less. Still, even when he started

making more money, there was never a question about who led the household. My mom simply allowed him to lead. She welcomed it.

"My father did what was best for us as opposed to himself. And while he wasn't working, he was pretty much a stay-at-home dad. So he cooked and everything like that. Then when he started working again, they shared those responsibilities. Yes, she'd submit to him, but he'd also submit to her in matters where she was an expert or where she was more qualified.

"So, growing up, I witnessed the way gender roles can be fluid despite the pressure or expectations of society."

And that's the thing—there are *so* many pressures and expectations—all pushing us and in different directions. Everything's a catch-22. No matter the decision you make, haters are gonna hate. Everyone's a critic. Whether or not you choose to submit, according to the rest of the world, you're darned if you do and you're darned if you don't.

"Some men just want a submissive woman, period. But I think submission is more of a reaction to the example the man has set. She'll submit only if he's proven that he's a leader, and a lot of Black women aren't immediately submissive—that's part of being the 'strong Black woman.'

"They've kind of been raised not to submit to anyone and forged by the fire, so it's definitely harder for Black women. There's also a lot of pressure on the man for him to be someone that his woman can submit to. Even once he's proven himself, it would still be up to her to submit or not. You can't force anyone to submit to you."

In the bible, Luke 12:48 states, *"To whom much is given, much is required."* That nugget of wisdom is a popular phrase even within the secular world. A lot of folks want to be granted such power or control. It feeds their ego. It makes them feel important. On the same token, *not* everyone wants to do the work and prove that they can handle the great deal of responsibility that may come with the role of the leader.

The irony is undeniable. The very people who come up with the rules are happy to do what they believe is their due diligence by regulating and enforcing the regimen. Yet those *same people* are also the ones who tend to bend the rules or challenge the integrity of their dynamics.

Regarding women who feel that they shouldn't have to pay bills and a man should be the sole provider, Odjo offered his take on the matter.

"Some people are like 'Oh, you can't have your cake and eat it too' because there are men who say, 'Well, why would I provide for someone who's not bringing anything to the table?' There's that push for reciprocity and a 'What are you doing for me?' mindset.

"But it's funny because men are the ones who put that power structure in place years ago [men provide, women submit]. The men in our generation are just expecting submission [without initially proving themselves as leaders]."

Odjo is more than willing to be the provider for his wife when the time comes. Given his example of love and partnership, it doesn't surprise me. Still, he also respects the fact that some women take pride in contributing and making money for themselves, which he says is perfectly fine as well. Finding a balance that is conducive to his and his wife's expectations and desires is what's most important for Odjo.

"I can provide anything she needs. I naturally would assume any financial responsibilities if we're married. The mortgage—bills like that. As the man that I am, if I'm able to assume the financial responsibilities 100 percent, then I would do so. That's just how I am. I feel like that's my duty as a husband. But let's just say I have an alpha wife and she has her own thing going and wants to take responsibility of whatever, then, of course, I'd accept that as well."

Odjo is a direct reflection of the old saying that swears that you can always tell how a man will treat his wife by the way he treats his mother. Odjo has a decent following on social media. All his close friends and followers alike can attest to the love and respect he has for his mother.

Odjo uploads little snapshots of himself cooking her delicious-looking meals and handing them directly to her as she's working on her computer or lounging on the couch. (I'm talking breakfast, lunch, dinner, or even a midnight snack—if she wants it, he will make sure that she gets it.) She sweetly blushes or thanks him for thinking of her. Also, when his mother is swamped with her work or her studies, he takes the initiative to run errands for her or takes her car to get it washed—and he does everything with a smile.

So, because of his dedication to his mother and how he lovingly shows his appreciation for her, he very much seems like the type of man who would cater to his wife as well and make sure that she too is well taken care of.

Odjo further stresses the point that he believes the roles of submission and provision shouldn't even be factors until he's married.

"Our generation has a lot of gray area in our relationships. We make stages for everything, but I think you're either single or you're in a relationship—point-blank. I think provision and submission should only be for marriage. Taking steps too prematurely can ruin the foundation.

"I don't need to talk about submission with a girl I'm dating because number one, I haven't even proven anything. Number two, we're probably not living together, so we're not sharing finances. We're not doing anything like that, so I don't think that should be in the question.

"I think provision and submission is a bridge that can be crossed if we're talking marriage. But any time before that, I think it kind of ruins certain aspects of marriage. Those are the things that make marriage sacred. That's what makes you two become one."

Two becoming one *does* have a nice *ring* to it—pun most certainly intended.

Anyway, on a serious note, in agreement with Odjo's point, the aspects of marriage should never be thrown into just another one of your flings.

Assuming certain responsibilities too soon or failing to clarify where the relationship is headed but still expecting submission or provision from your partner could lead to awkward situations down the road.

Chapter 12

Greg: The "Father First"

Remember when I said earlier how hard it was for me to find single Black men to interview?

Well, Greg, 34, was a perfect stranger who showed up at my apartment one day.

Not randomly or without reason—that would be creepy.

Greg was a maintenance man at the apartments I was living at. He was responding to a work-order ticket that I had submitted for my fridge.

Like I said, I was discouraged because of how difficult it was for me to find another eligible interview subject. So naturally, I asked God to somehow send me another single man.

Next thing I knew, there was a knock on my door. (Won't he do it?)

While he was working on my fridge, Greg and I had small talk that somehow led to the topic of my book. I told him I was looking for single Black men who were eager to have a conversation with me about relationships and gender norms.

Greg instantly voiced his interest in being a part of this project, and I'm glad for that as he presented a much-different angle than the other men I spoke with prior to him.

A dedicated single father, Greg proudly expressed his devotion to his kids. Even though he admittedly didn't have the best examples for an ideal relationship between man and woman, he did appreciate the bond that his mother and father shared.

Greg's father had other children from previous marriages, but it didn't affect the way his mom and dad took care of him. He appreciated how they respected each other. Even when his parents weren't romantically involved, they kept the kids as their number one priority.

Watching his parents interact with each other shaped his views and his behavior as a young adult. He told me about the dynamic of his parents' relationship.

"I'm not even gonna lie to you—watching my parents made me feel like certain things were okay because I saw what they did and, in my eyes, it was working. I didn't think anything was wrong with it. My mom and dad were together when they had me, but they weren't married. A few years later, they had my brother and broke up shortly after he was born. But they were still friends. I remember my dad always being there.

"My dad used to keep all his kids, when I was growing up, as long as the other mothers wasn't trippin'. He always came to my mom's house to take me and my brother to school three days a week—whether he had to catch the bus or borrow my mom's car. He's been down bad—all types of stuff. My mom never kicked him while he was down."

Greg witnessed his father navigate life with a total of eight kids that he shared between three women. Soon, Greg became a father himself. He found out his then girlfriend was pregnant; she was eighteen years old. He reflected on the time he broke it off with her, his first child's mother, before she gave birth to their son.

"I told her we don't have to be together to raise our son. I said, 'My mom and dad did it, and they were fine.' Initially, we were together. We were high school sweethearts, but I was young and dumb, and I wanted to do whatever I wanted to do. I wanted to break up with her, so I used my parents' situation to persuade her that we'd be good too.

"But telling an eighteen-year-old who's been with you for the past four years that you want to break up when they're having your

child? It's like 'Oh, you don't wanna be with me now? And you're telling me we'll be good because your mom and dad was good?' She was heartbroken. She made me swallow those words. She's married now—has beautiful kids and a wonderful husband that I get along with that's amazing with my son."

As a single father to two young boys, Greg's angle on provision and submission is mainly in favor of his kids. As a matter of fact, throughout the entire interview, he had the almost-automatic tendency to revert the topic back to his children. It made me think, *Maybe he really doesn't have the desire to be in a relationship. Maybe a relationship is literally the furthest thing from his mind.*

"Me and both of my kids' moms are on real good terms. I'm not on child support. To me, it's nothing to take care of my kids. I give a certain amount of money every month to my oldest son's mother, and then me and my youngest son's mother choose to just split everything and take turns buying food, Pampers—things like that."

All in all, Greg believes his only obligation as a grown man is to ensure his kids are taken care of. Greg doesn't believe he's obligated to provide for his woman—whether he's married or not. Instead, he feels he's *responsible* for providing for the *children* that he and his woman share.

"I don't think a man is supposed to be the type of provider who just comes in, sweeps you off your feet, and assumes all the financial responsibility. To me, as a provider, what I'm supposed to do is take care of my kids.

Meaning, if anything happens, I'll be the first point of contact.

"For instance, if the car breaks down, call me, and I'll come and take care of it. MFs will try to rip you off. Being a provider works both ways. I'm not coming to take on more responsibility. As a provider, I'm coming to aid."

The word "contribute" is defined by the *Merriam-Webster Dictionary* as follows: "to give or supply (something, such as money or time) as a part or share."

That definition alone exemplifies Greg's standpoint when it comes to relationships. He feels it's fairer to *share* the responsibilities. Greg believes it's most beneficial to *share* the weight of the bills and other financial obligations and *supplement* each other's income.

"I would want us to both be employed and financially stable [as individuals]. As a man and a provider, she wants me to be reliable, but I would want to be able to rely on my woman as well. In marriage, if we have kids, of course I'm going to do all that a man and a father can. We're both going to be paying bills.

"You had bills before you met me. I mean, yeah, if I'm fortunate enough where I'm making more money, then I wouldn't mind doing that [paying most of the bills]. But if I'm taking a load off you, I'd also need you to take a load off of me."

Greg is a prime example of how we mimic what we witnessed while growing up. My theory is, there are two main reasons why Greg isn't necessarily dead set on spoiling his woman or, in his words, "sweeping her off her feet."

The first reason is simply because he never witnessed his own mother being swept off her feet by his father. Certain characteristics or behaviors may not come naturally to someone who's never observed them.

What he did observe was a man being completely dedicated to raising his kids and being an integral part of their lives. He spoke to me about how he feels the media views Black men—not just how it views Black men as providers but how it views them in general.

"They don't really see us as providers. The rhetoric that's commonly thrown around is 'There's a few good men out there.' People don't find it unusual if Black men are single. It's not unusual when people find out 'Oh, it didn't work out between him and his kids' mother.'

"Us being providers or just doing the right thing—for instance, starting a business, marrying a woman, raising a kid with her—stuff like that—people don't expect that. So now, things we'd be praised for are weaponized against us. Now, it's pushed for women to do their own thing—don't depend on a man for anything.

"That's kind of why I'm starting to go along with that narrative. I had to adjust to what's normal now—women taking care of things

on their own—not afraid to speak up for themselves and be their own muscle.

"That's why I don't feel like women must be submissive and I must be the provider. I mean, I'm never going to sit back and let a woman take care of me unless I'm sick and unable to work for myself."

Greg also gave his input on how, although there's still long a way to go, the perception of Black men is beginning to transform into something more positive:

"In the media, Black men aren't usually seen as great fathers, good friends, or hard workers—that's not what the narrative has been. In the past, 'good Black men' weren't celebrated as much, but these days, I see we are being publicly recognized and appreciated more often."

No matter what society or the media may circulate, Greg says he's got no problem with keeping himself grounded and having a mind of his own:

"The media doesn't affect my views. On my social media, I'll post my children every day and other random things. The media is just for fun. But I do get a lot of praise just for having my kids. But it's like, they're my kids—of course I have them. I try not to be negative when people say certain things, but people are surprised that I have a great relationship with my kids even though I'm not with either of their mothers."

Greg's dating style or expectation seems to do away with the traditional gender norms altogether. He feels there should be more of an emphasis on the contribution between two partners within a relationship. He and his woman would ideally contribute in terms of not only provision but submission as well.

"As far as submission, we both should be willing to give in and accept certain things from one another. I think both the man and woman should have equal parts of submission. I don't really think all women should have to be submissive. Some women will not submit in any form or fashion, but that doesn't mean they don't deserve to be married."

On the other hand, the essence of being a provider involves being a true leader. Greg was honest enough to admit that until he reaches a better place in life for himself, he will not be in the position to add value to someone else's life.

I felt that on a personal level. Being secure in who you are sets the tone for your relationship. I told Greg I was happy with being alone. I expressed to him how I finally found contentment and peace in my singlehood because I was pouring all my love and my energy into bettering myself *for myself.* I felt liberated and affirmed all on my own, and I thanked God for getting me to that place.

It made me think of being on a flight. Before the plane takes off, the speaker over the intercom tells you that in case the oxygen levels drop, you should put on your own breathing mask before you try to help anyone else with theirs. Otherwise, you're not going to be much help to them since you'll both be gasping for air.

The older I got, the more I began to realize that, just as much as some women expect a man to have it all together by the time he reaches a woman, a lot of men feel as though they are better off being alone if they aren't where they want to be in life—no matter how much they may like a woman. Women may feel this way too, but men especially.

I say this because as I listened to Greg talk, it made me reflect on the times I had openly expressed my interest in a man who seemed as though he was extremely interested in me, but then he would suddenly become withdrawn because he felt I was moving too fast. A couple of them expressed how they had other goals and endeavors that they'd like to accomplish before they became exclusive with anyone.

Then, there were the countless stories I'd heard from my girlfriends about how a man was a totally different person when his career was up in the air or if he were faced with any kind of financial adversity. These men displayed everything from irrationality to becoming aggressive or easily irritable and, in more extreme cases, flat out initiating a breakup when things were otherwise going perfectly fine.

Whether it was really how they felt or they just used the same tired excuses as scapegoats to get what they want and get ghost, we may never know.

Either way, I was glad when Greg gave me this insight. It made me think that perhaps he's not the only man who genuinely feels the way he does. Maybe a lot of men do, but for the fear of being too harshly judged or, worse, emasculated, they shut down and shy away from relationships altogether—only entertaining flings, one-night stands, or even long-standing friends with benefits or situationships.

"You've articulated exactly how I feel and the things I'm working on. That's why I'm not in a relationship. How can I be in a relationship if I ain't ready to lead? It made me feel inadequate in relationships because it was an insecurity of mine."

Having children puts your mind in perspective to take care of them and make sure they're provided for by any means. Your goals and dreams must take a back seat—including being in a relationship. Greg, much like many others, realized he had to do what he had to do for the sake of his children. He said that he settled into his maintenance career. His job may not be buying designer bags and financing trips with women, but it's what's been feeding his kids. And I have the utmost respect for that.

Greg is keeping his goals and dreams in mind for his future.

"I've always known what I wanted to do since I was seventeen years old. I wanted to do heating and cooling, but I ended up settling for maintenance. Well, now I'm getting my own property. I'm setting up more long-term things so that when the time comes, I can be more suitable for my partner. I can add to what they already have going on, and vice versa."

Regardless of whether he sees himself being with someone long-term, Greg says his standards are simple:

"I wouldn't entertain anyone who doesn't have something going for their self. Anybody around me has to have goals and be respectable. I have to think highly of you."

A young, dedicated Black dad whose main focus is to raise and spend time with his children isn't rare or unheard of. Like Greg said, it's just not acknowledged enough simply because, unfortunately, negativity and nonsense are more intriguing than what's wholesome and uplifting.

Domestic Partnerships

Chapter 13

Charles and Alycia—The Dutiful Dad and the Money-Making Mom

When the foundation of a relationship is built on trust, the bond that you and your significant other share is virtually unbreakable. However, the key to building such strong trust is matching your actions with your words.

We all have expectations within relationships. The desires we express should correspond with our verbalized points of view; otherwise, things become downright confusing.

Meet Charles, 29, and Alycia, 28.

This couple, who just recently got engaged, understands how imperative it is for their beliefs to mirror not just their expectations but their behaviors as well.

Charles and Alycia have been together for seven years and share two beautiful kids together, who just so happen to be my niece and nephew.

Okay, okay! Charles is my older brother. Him being the stubborn yet socially reluctant ram that he is, he wasn't too enthusiastic about speaking with me at first. Come to find out, that was only because he wasn't clear on the concept of the book and he thought I was *seeking relationship advice* from *him*.

After learning this, we all, including Alycia, laughed together.

But seriously, I'm glad he and Alycia both agreed to share their points of view because they opened my eyes to a question I had for the longest time, yet I couldn't quite articulate it. I'll tell you my question in a minute, but first, let me tell you what triggered it: Alycia's take on submission.

"Nobody was worried about being submissive. At first, all our generation of women cared about was being on their own. There are lots of women who think independently, and they don't feel like they need to be submissive to a man because they're already so independent."

That's when my question popped in my head: Are the same women who are independent and anti-submission also the ones who expect a man to spoil them or take care of them? On the other hand, are the men who expect natural submission from their women the same men who don't feel obligated to provide for their women—no matter how financially stable or wealthy they are?

If this is the case, this contradictory behavior is the main culprit to failing relationships.

Some women are braggadocios, going on and on about how they're self-made, and they're openly against women being submissive. But some of these women are the same ones who have expectations of being showered in gifts and trips and having a man feel obligated to pay their bills.

And vice versa.

There are men who complain about how women don't listen, won't cook, won't clean, etc., yet these are the same men who want to go fifty-fifty on the bills or question a woman's integrity if she feels she shouldn't have to contribute as much financially.

Friends, I'll say it simply: Your relationship cannot work that way.

Life will put you in a position where your values and principles are put to the test, and they must match your anticipations.

And Charles made his values clear regarding being a provider for Alycia and their children.

"To me, being a provider means to be the man of the house. He's the leader. He takes care of the bills and protects the house and his family."

Charles wasn't afraid to practice what he preached either.

After Alycia gave birth to my niece, finding a new job wasn't easy. Charles told her not to worry about finding work. Exploring her entrepreneurial desires was weighing on her mind, but now she had a daughter to care for.

Charles encouraged her to stay home full-time and take care of their daughter while he continued to work every day. As the lead mechanic at his job, money was good, and work was steady. So he had no problem with the mother of his child staying at home while he took care of them. Charles reflected on what drove his ambition and hard-work ethic to take care of himself, Alycia, and their infant.

"I mean, growing up and watching my dad, I felt like even if it takes not being home and enduring hard times, or whatever the situation may be, you gotta basically be a superhero. The man is the one who takes care of any situation—no matter what. He makes sacrifices. Even if it means working late, not being able to spend time with your family as much as you'd like. If your wife is out of work, even if that's hard on you, you gotta accept it and make sacrifices. That's the key word—'sacrifices.'"

After six months of being a stay-at-home mom, Alycia finally found another steady position. It was the first time in her adult life that she had been without work for so long. Before and after she and my brother got together, she was always used to having her own money, and she took pride in her workmanship and independence.

Yet Alycia understands that some women would rather be fully maintained by their men—no matter what. This isn't necessarily wrong; it just wasn't Alycia's style.

Charles says a woman's submission depends on her perception of her man.

"I think 80 to 90 percent of Black women will be submissive if she's with someone she views as powerful."

Alycia followed up with her point of view on some women of our generation and their desires:

"A lot of women just look for financial security. They just want somebody to take care of them. But I don't know if it's in regard to loving their man or just having him. To make matters worse, provision is shown more from a celebrity standpoint. Some people didn't have a two-parent household to demonstrate what it truly means to provide and submit."

Ah, yes, Alycia—I know what you mean. Gossip columns post how this celebrity gifted their partner a Mercedes-Benz for their birthday or that celebrity dropped fifty thousand dollars on some bling for their partner on Valentine's Day and so on and so forth.

This high-class perception of provision is held to a much greater standard than it should be, and this is some people's only example of the term.

Charles says this is why social media and the lives of certain celebrities are not good examples of what provision truly means.

"Social media has a negative effect on people who aren't in tune with reality. It idolizes relationships that just look perfect."

In other words, no one really broadcasts the negative side of a relationship. Of course not! But the cute pictures in the matching pajamas, filming the exchange of luxurious gifts, and my all-time favorite, pics of sitting across from each other on their private jet are the things we see.

Now, the infidelity, toxicity, abuse, etc.—those things aren't so much in the spotlight. And even when they are, people keep up with all the drama because they're celebrities, and famous people have a way of making *everything* look good to certain people.

Social media is a monster of a medium. There are 7.7 billion people in the world, and approximately half of them (3.81 billion) use a personal or social online platform. There's an old wise saying: "Comparison is the thief of joy." That's because when we compare, there are two possible outcomes: we either develop the feeling of inferiority or the feeling of superiority. Lots of people are getting high off the latter, while the rest are suffering from the former.

Millennials are slowly but surely beginning to realize that social media is great for many things, but measuring our worth based off what our followers are posting or experiencing is stealing our joy. As a matter of fact, it's making many people depressed.

A few years back, in 2018, a study was conducted, which included 143 students from the University of Pennsylvania. The students were randomly split into two groups: Group A had limited social media (only thirty minutes per day for three weeks), and Group B had unlimited access for three weeks.

I think you know where this is going, but if you don't—surprise!

Group B showed a significant increase in depression and loneliness in comparison to Group A.

I mean, think about it: Can you imagine how much happier you'd be if you only spent 3.5 hours per week on social media as opposed to spending that same amount of time or more every day—like how some folks do without even thinking about it? Next time we have the urge to grab our phones and binge-scroll, we should take that into consideration.

Chapter 14

Chris and Val—The Loving and Laid-Back Couple

The Black community is already challenged by systemic racial oppression dating back to what seems like the beginning of time. The phrase "systemic racism" is often used; however, not all of us have a clear understanding of what it is. Just to clarify, this term refers to systems and structures put in place that have procedures or processes that purposely disadvantage African Americans.

When you pair systemic racial oppression with the damaging rhetoric that annoyingly aims to pinpoint "why" Black women aren't as submissive as their White counterparts, you get a recipe for resentment and unsuccessful relationships.

Right off the bat, Val, 28, gave me some straightforward yet striking insight on Black women's dilemma regarding submission. Her longtime boyfriend and the father of her two children is Chris, 27.

"I feel like a lot of Black women do want to be submissive, but they don't have a man that makes them comfortable being submissive to. If the man was providing for her and being supportive of her, then her submission would come easily. But there are some men who expect their woman to submit, but they won't because the man is not up to par."

I must agree with Val on this 100 percent. Black women often get a bad rap for being difficult or ornery, but the truth is, they're fed so much contradictory advice from society and family, they must make decisions and fend for themselves in ways that make them look like the villains. Oftentimes, this leads to the use of nonconformist mindsets as means for survival—not every man for himself but *every Black woman for herself.*

A 1965 government report entitled *The Negro Family: The Case for National Action*, also known as *The Moynihan Report*, is responsible for further perpetuating the idea that households led by Black women are Black America's biggest downfall.

While marriage is a noble life achievement to strive for, we must quickly dispose of the habit of teaching young women that it is more important to *be chosen* by any means—even if you must shrink yourself and use your voice less often. Instead, we should be encouraging them to take advantage of not only *their power to choose* but also *their ability to make wise decisions.*

It's true that a healthy union between two people can provide an abundance of security and contentment. However, what's problematic is the underlying notion that some folks have that brainwashes some women into believing that they must accept the bare minimum or downplay their own achievements (or, worse, try not to "overachieve" or become "too successful" so they won't intimidate potential suitors) in order to be more desirable. This is what's causing the attitude coming from Black women who are sick of the misogyny and breathing more life into Black machismo.

Val then talked about what it takes to earn a woman's submission.

"If you want me to be submissive, you've gotta play your part. You've gotta do everything you're supposed to do. If a Black woman has a man who stays at home, doesn't work, doesn't take care of the kids—is she really supposed to submit to that? No."

Another unhealthy ideal of traditional marriage ties a man's value to his income, positioning him to be the dominant figure in the household without question. Chris says that it needs to be more than the money that a man brings to the table, and regardless of how much money he brings in, a man still shouldn't expect a woman to be happy with a dictatorship instead of a relationship.

"As a man, it doesn't have to be like 'Everything I say goes.' I think our modern generation of women isn't afraid to use their voice, and their opinions matter more than what people were used to back in the day."

Let me just say here that both Chris and Val were raised in Black woman–led households. At this point, you may already be able to tell how levelheaded these two are. That just goes to show you that, contrary to what was stated in the government report, they are using their upbringings to help them make wiser decisions as adults.

As a matter of fact, Chris and Val effortlessly exemplify what a happy, healthy relationship between two young parents should look like—regardless of what they witnessed while growing up. Chris explained his point of view when it comes to people using bad examples as excuses for their bad adult behaviors.

"When you're a kid, you don't really know what grown people have going on, but still, you just know it ain't right. So as you get older, you ask yourself, 'Do I wanna do what they did, knowing it was wrong, or do I wanna go down a different path?' But people use the bad examples they had growing up as an excuse.

"When things go wrong, they blame those who came before them, saying 'My mom did it. My dad did it.' But I think, 'Okay, so what does that have to do with you?' You see your parents doing something and you know it ain't right, then keep that in mind. It ain't right."

It's natural for us to want examples or role models. But the main point that Chris was getting at was the importance of being mindful of what you accept as okay, and if it's up to you to break a generational cycle, then be disciplined and mature enough to do so—no excuses. Role models and #RelationshipGoals aren't wrong; however, what matters is being careful not to lose sight of what's *right*.

There are many popular celebrity couples who lots of people, millennials especially, tend to idolize and for no good reason. Val feels that the celebrities who are worthy of admiration are the ones we don't hear from enough.

"I like LeBron and Savannah. I love them. But they're not in the limelight. J. Cole and his wife, they're not in the limelight. Kendrick Lamar and his wife, they're not in the limelight. I don't even know what she looks like.

"The celebrities who may have a positive impact on social media are the ones who don't want to be a part of it because it's so negative. The media just has a negative impact on relationships."

Val's right. Many of the millennials' idols or the couples they've put on a pedestal have major fallings-out, and before you know it, the same people who were idolizing the relationships end up being the ones throwing stones when things go wrong, further instigating the allegations.

Much like the low-key celebs they admire, Chris and Val aren't always on social media either, sharing every waking moment of their lives, their innermost thoughts, or what they're currently at odds about. They understand that there's a time and a place for everything; it's never a good time to make social media the place to air out all your business.

Chris and Val exude an aura of serenity—cool but calm and sure of themselves, confident in their love and their partnership. That's the peace of mind that comes with keeping some things personal and choosing what you don't mind sharing with the world. Everything else, they keep to themselves.

Chapter 15

Mike and Shak—The Two Peas in a Pod

While still on the subject of social media, meet Mike, 47, and Shak, 48.

In the era of Facebook and Instagram—where there're memes, opinion pieces, and photos galore—for some folks, it's easy to get caught up in the whirlwind of cyberspace—all things good, bad, and ugly.

People post their unsolicited advice and uneducated, asinine points of view, which has absolutely no merit nine times out of ten.

For these reasons alone, many people pay little to no mind to their social media feeds as they're attention hogs and emotional triggers waiting to be pulled.

Shak says she's mindful of her social media intake, careful not to internalize what she sees.

"Social media makes you judgmental sometimes, but it doesn't necessarily change my views."

Mike, on the other hand, pointed out that there's actually—get this—a silver lining to social media. Mostly raised by his grandparents and having to cope with his father's lack of attendance, Mike is thankful for the one thing that he feels social media is starting to get right: creating a platform that shines a beautiful light on Black fatherhood.

"For a long time, the perception was that we didn't provide. I can honestly say, one blessing from social media is how the world can see now that we're excellent fathers and great providers. When I was

growing up, the picture society painted was we're all deadbeat dads, not taking care of our families. That was the ongoing perception.

"But social media helped Black men a whole lot because it shows the truth. People see there are lots of us out here handling our responsibilities for our families."

The way we receive our information has experienced quite the evolution over the years, so we're exposed to even more points of view and contradictory opinions, and they're all literally at our fingertips. The television was invented in1927. This is how many watched the racially charged woes, targeted epidemics, and national emergencies that America's crooked and corrupt government is solely responsible for.

Computers, however, were just gaining popularity and becoming an easily attainable yet sophisticated technology, starting to be present in most family households by the 1980s. Not long after computers were being purchased on a mainstream level, we realized they can be used for much more than business purposes; Americans were also introduced to blogging in the late 1980s. So now, not only could they chat, which began in 1988, ten years later, users could upload pictures and congregate online.

It wasn't until the early 2000s when we were introduced to Myspace, the social media OG, and, finally, Facebook.

The point that I'm making is, social media is relatively new. It was only sixteen years ago when Facebook and Twitter became available on the worldwide web.

Everything happened so fast and progressed so quickly, we really didn't know how overwhelmed and, frankly, obsessed we'd become once social media became the predominant medium.

In terms of social media sharing more positive points of view regarding Black fatherhood, Shak agrees with Mike. However, she feels the lack of provision is mainly viewed as a problem of the younger generation of Black men—for instance, men who became teen fathers and are now ages 20 to 30.

"I think society often stereotypes younger men as not being providers. They were taking older men into consideration in terms of their views of Black men as providers. They feel the younger

generation isn't as stable with their women and their children. They're just seen as baby daddies."

If these same baby daddies are products of nonexistent relationships with their own fathers, that is more than likely the problem. There are some men who remember the sting of the empty void their fathers left them with, and so they unfortunately follow suit when they have children of their own, shamelessly bastardizing their offspring.

On the other hand, there are men like Mike; since he didn't have the best circumstances while growing up or the best relationship with his own father, it gave him more reason to be present in his son's life—and not just present but a constant and positive driving force to his well-being and success.

"I grew up in the projects in a single-parent household. That showed me what I didn't want in life. As a child, I used to wish I could spend more time with my dad—especially as I started getting older and making important decisions. I see where our lack of communication with one another could have helped me in my life, growing up.

"Since I didn't see my dad as much, it made me make sure, when I had a son, I'd be in his life. I said to myself, 'You know how it felt without your father. You don't want your son to feel that way.'"

Taking your pain and making sure you don't inflict the same type of pain on someone else is a very noble decision to make. Damaging people you love and blaming your indiscretions and lack of maturity on others is toxic behavior, period.

So, all in all, given Mike's experiences and observations throughout his childhood, he feels the role of being a partner and a father is very straightforward:

"As the man of the house, you gotta provide everything. Provide protection, and as the backbone of the family, provide comfort."

At this point, Shak chimed in, saying, "I like that answer." So even though this generation is dead set on the financial aspect of provision, Shak believes there's so much more to it than that.

Shak also believes in the traditional gender norms, where she's submissive to her man in a healthy and respectable manner and she can rely on him to provide for their family physically and financially.

"Men handle the household as far as bills and repairs. Yes, we can split some bills, but usually, the man pays the bills as the provider. For instance, if I'm not working, then he'll handle it."

Provision and submission are not supposed to be thoughtless transactions (e.g., bring her the money, and she'll be obedient).

Ideally, submission and provision are two necessary aspects of any normal relationship. But Shak believes Black women are stereotyped as too demanding and aren't seen as submissive unless a man is out earning them.

"Oh my goodness, people think we aren't submissive at all. Society sees us as too headstrong, especially when the woman makes more than the man. Some people really don't expect Black women to submit if she's making more money than her man."

To this, Mike responded bluntly,

"If a woman is willing to submit because she knows she can get a Birkin for her birthday, then her submission is being bought."

And this is a relationship that a lot of people don't mind. There's a phrase I've seen (on social media) that says, "This generation is more interested in looking successful than actually being successful."

Where's the lie? A life of perfection looks good for all our followers and those we're trying to impress. As I said before, we get so caught up in looking good, we're not putting in the work to be all that we post to be.

Mike believes that most of the time, people's picture-perfect lifestyles and relationships are all fronts.

"Social media is a gift and a curse. Everybody can be 'great' on social media—whether it's true or not. Anyone can give off the impression that they're great."

And this is what's been contributing to the unrealistic goals that we kill ourselves to reach.

Chapter 16

Rai and Olivia—The Linguistic and Artistic

I'm not quite sure where to begin with this complementary duo. They're both so sophisticated and mature yet down-to-earth and simplistic. Rai, 32, is seven years Olivia's senior, which of course makes her 25. Both are gifted dancers too. So not only do these two share the same incredible talent, but after conducting this interview, I realized they also share the same intellect, which is apparently what makes them mesh so well.

Although Rai is several years older than his girlfriend, Olivia, he's aware of what type of grown woman he's been blessed with. He knows she's wise enough to hold her own, strong enough to fend for herself, and responsible enough to make important decisions for her life. One of those important decisions, as a matter of fact, was to move to California with him so that they could pursue their dance careers in a more affluent and talented town—one that would offer them each more consistent and legitimate opportunities.

Olivia knew from the beginning that Rai has the utmost respect for her. Not to be confused with those creepy older men—you know the kind I'm talking about—the old lowlifes who prey on women who are much younger than they are, hoping to manipulate or victimize them and take advantage of their naivety.

Rai is the complete opposite. He acknowledges Olivia for the woman that she is—even to the point of insisting that he must work for her submission by proving he's capable of meeting her requirements of provision.

"Submission is something that I feel like I, as a man, would have to earn. I don't think I should just automatically get her submission because what if I'm not fulfilling everything she'd need to feel comfortable submitting to me?"

A thought-provoking question—one that I'd assumed was rhetorical based off Olivia's remarks in terms of Rai's natural sense of responsibility. Rai's attitude toward being a provider for his woman and his work ethic stems from what he witnessed while growing up.

Rai was raised mostly by his grandparents and was inspired by the dynamic of their relationship and how they interacted with each other. As mentioned in the previous chapters, older men such as the fathers and grandfathers of millennials were more prone to following traditional norms, which meant being the providers for their families and meant assuming most, if not all, the financial responsibilities.

Older men worked their butts off in their prime and even when they were getting up in age to keep their loved ones comfortable and well taken care of-whether the woman of the house was working or not. Rai reflected on his grandfather's work ethic:

"My grandfather definitely provided. He was a janitor back in the day—at Children's Hospital in Oakland—and at another hospital in Oakland, he was the custodial manager.

"He was also into real estate and is a property owner. He had other skills and always had a side hustle. If one of the doctors was going out of town and they needed somebody to take care of their horses, they'd call my grandfather. If somebody needed some yard work done, they'd call my grandfather.

"He was always there to provide for my grandmother, but at the same time, my grandmother was a registered nurse."

Although Rai's grandmother was bringing in plenty of money on her own, he insisted that his grandfather still made it his business—literally—to make sure she was taken care of.

"The goal was to always keep the woman on her throne as the queen of the house. It's not so much a Eurocentric perspective of

patriarchy but more of a matrilineal situation where the man has full power and the woman has full power, and they bring all their power together at the end of the day to take care of business."

Rai is an old soul—not just in the obvious way by how he's a bit older than Olivia but to the point that you can tell that he was brought up by people who instilled those values in him at a young age, and they stuck with him in his adulthood. Our younger generation would have better relationships if we valued teamwork the way the generations before us did—when there was a sense of simplicity and responsibility.

Each partner would gladly make up for what the other lacked. Things were handled dutifully and respectfully. There was more of a give-and-take within partnerships back in the day that didn't need as much explanation as we do today.

It's no one's fault. Times change, but we can't let the changes of the seasons make us forget what's truly important: looking out for each other. Rai witnessed the respectable and functional partnership of his grandparents while growing up.

"I grew up in a household where there was a lot of teamwork. My grandmother was more educated on certain things, whereas my grandfather was well versed and educated on other things. So they'd each put in work wherever they were the strongest.

"For example, if my grandfather needed help reading something or making sure his contracts were right for his real estate, he'd always check with my grandmother.

"It was expected that the man was supposed to work hard so that if the woman wanted to relax or retire or not work for the season, she could do that. I think the man should do his best to provide the woman the option of changing up her schedule if she wants to for her own comfort."

Olivia and Rai are both blessed with amazing dance opportunities year-round. However, they have full-time jobs in addition to dancing. Rai is a karate and taekwondo instructor to kids, and Olivia is a brand ambassador.

While they both contribute to paying bills and keeping up with their financial responsibilities within their domestic partnership, Olivia believes it may not be as realistic for Rai to take on the role of the sole provider for their household. However, she's thankful for his desire to do so, and it makes her respect Rai even more:

"Right now, I think Rai keeps trying to do that—provide for the both of us. But I won't let him. Rai and I are not married, and we don't necessarily share all our money at this point. We do share some responsibilities like groceries. Or if I need help with a bill or if Rai needs help with a bill—whoever's got it at that time, we'll help each other.

"But because we're still trying to get established out here, sometimes I have more expendable income or my paycheck just happened to fall on the right time—we're just helping each other right now, but Rai has more of a predictable 'provider' pay schedule.

"Rai maintains that he wants to make it easy for me to do my own thing sometimes, but I don't like accepting that and feeling like I'm totally dependent on his check, but it's nice to know he at least cares."

Knowing this is enough to make it easier for her to submit to Rai as the head of the household—regardless of what type of money each of them brings in. Olivia says it's not just about money; she believes the decision to submit as a woman is based more on a man's mindset, behavior, and level of wisdom.

"Contrary to popular belief, a lot of women want to submit to their man. But women also want to be independent. Still, I feel like women want someone who's worthy of being submitted to. No one wants to follow the lead of someone who's corny, you know? Show me that you're a competent leader because who wants to be following someone who's out there looking like a fool?"

Now don't get it confused. Olivia is aware of how society often perceives Black women as more difficult or attitudinal than the members of other races. Still, in no way, shape, or form does Olivia believe that her justification for *her* comfort in being submissive to *her man* should mean that *all* women must submit or become more lenient and completely let their guards down. As a matter of fact, Olivia feels that

Black women have legitimate reasons as to why they have reservations when it comes to submission.

"It's like a double standard. Generationally in America, Black women have had to be so 'strong' for a wide variety of reasons within Black marriages. Whether it was because of Black men systematically being dragged out of the house or just financial oppression, we've had to be 'strong.' Yet you have—in my opinion— annoying Black men on social media saying things like 'Why are Black women so stubborn?' or 'Why don't Black women want to submit?'

"It's not that Black women don't want to be that way [able to conform or submit more easily in this day and age]. It's just that we've had no choice but to be that way for so long. The nerve of you even saying, 'How come you can't be more submissive like White women or Asian women?'

"Sorry for this language, but I'm like, bitch, we've been dragged through the mud with you guys for years. How dare you ask me to be more docile?"

Rai says his provision isn't dependent on her complete submission either way. It's more about maintaining his respect and level of trustworthiness while still acknowledging all that his woman is capable of with or without him.

"As a man, I'm always gonna want to do everything for my woman, but I'm not gonna pretend like she has no power, strength, or talent that God's given her too, you know?"

Rai's upbringing was slightly different from Olivia's as he was raised primarily by his grandparents. He says his parents were caught up in the drug epidemic and, in turn, were in and out of jail. Olivia, on the other hand, comes from a two-parent household—one with a Black mother and a Mexican father. Each of her parents has found major success in their respective industries and, in turn, made a beautiful, wealthy life for Olivia and her younger sister. But some hardships are bound to happen and simply cannot be avoided.

Olivia reflected on what she remembered had happened between her parents when they went through a bit of a rough patch—just as most normal families do. Although the capability to take on all or most of the financial responsibilities is often associated with provision, the perception can be harmful if one feels they aren't able to do so as much as they'd like to.

"Machismo" is described as a strong or aggressive masculine pride, and it has stronger precedence within Hispanic culture. Olivia reflected on her father's outlook in contrast to the amount of respect the family always had for him even during hard times:

"I was raised in a family that really emphasized men as providers. Of course, it wasn't like women couldn't bring anything to the table, but it was non-negotiable that the man of the house had to provide. Obviously, money is the main expectation, but also food, a home—tangible things.

"It wasn't so much the emotional part, but when I hear men as providers, I definitely think of my dad. But if something happened to his job or his money, it seemed like he would feel less important— which totally wasn't true—but he would feel less important to the family structure because he wasn't doing the provider thing the way he thought he was supposed to."

Black men and Hispanic men especially identify with machismo and defining themselves by what they're able to provide and their level of physical strength as the protector of a family.

"Even though I've had nice, successful, loving Black men in my life, my own father is not Black. While he is very close to the Black community, at the end of the day, he's not a Black man.

"So sometimes when I look at the way he treats their marriage, he definitely comes from a slightly different point of view, and I think that point of view is a little more male-dominated. I think he's beginning to loosen up more the older he gets. He's sixty now, and he seems less hypermasculine in their marriage."

Rai and Olivia experienced different situational instances with their upbringings, yet their values still coincide, which is the beauty of the evolved millennial. We recognize each other's differences, but we don't resent each other for them or make demands or belittle the one who just can't get it "right."

Instead, we embrace each other's good *and* bad, and we do what we can to be all that we can be to each other.

Rai explained his perspective in terms of his duty to protect and being the man of the house:

"Because the world is crazy and we do still live in a patriarchal-led society and I don't want Olivia to have to deal with any knuckleheads, I think I should be the head of the household in terms of being the bones and the skull.

"I'll receive all the blunt force and the damage, and if anything crazy comes our way, it'll be on my head. But the actual thinking, like the brain, I think she should be one side and I'll be the other side. So we're both the brain, but I'm the skull."

At this point, I was in awe at how beautifully he articulated his ideal dynamic of a relationship between a man and a woman. While this is how some would say we should be, men and women are at odds instead. It's not just the way we grew up or our past traumas. Rai believes it also has a lot to do with the music we listen to and the messages of the artists.

"Most of the music you hear where they're speaking about women is coming from that 'I was just a boy yesterday,' young-man mindset, including some of these guys in their thirties and forties. Just because you're a certain age doesn't mean you've matured past certain things. I get really annoyed.

"On one hand, I get it. I was eighteen, twenty-one years old before. But it seems like all the music is coming from that young-boy or young-man stage. That's all you hear is a young man's perspective. You don't hear enough music that's from a grown man or an older man's perspective. Even the male view is limited among male views."

On the other hand, Olivia says social media plays a role. It seems to try to deliver a message of unity or at least spark respectable dialogue, but the gossip columns and popular Instagram pages always seem to miss the mark.

"The media is always trying to get us to talk about provision and submission, but I feel like it's always two steps behind. I feel like the memes and social accounts I see are always prompting debates about things my friends and I already discussed years ago.

"The media's trying to help us talk about it, but so many of us are on a different page, and that's why we always end up yelling at each other in the comments. Some of us have already gotten to a point where we understand certain historical contexts or have reached a certain level of self-awareness.

"Then, there are some of us who are in the 'relationship sunken place.' So I think while the media is trying to help us have good conversation, because so many of us in the comments are coming from so many different places [emotionally, mentally, spiritually], we just aren't understanding each other. So, in a weird way, social media is trying to help us, but instead, it's hurting us."

Olivia and Rai are right. Knowledge is power. Yet we give so much of it away when we let ourselves be pacified by the distraction of social media. We need more in-person forums, face-to-face discussions, therapy sessions, and genuine and open dialogue—not to throw shade but to seek an understanding. Online methods are convenient for some cases, but some objectives are much better achieved in person—not from behind our computer screens or in the comment sections on Instagram and Facebook.

Married Couples

Chapter 17

Malik and Bri—The Young Love

They're both followers of Christ. They happily subscribe to the greater half of traditional gender norms—how the woman submits, and the man is the leader of the household and provides. They've been together for eight years and completed marriage counseling before they tied the knot. They'll soon be celebrating their second wedding anniversary.

And they're only twenty-four and twenty-five years old.

So much wisdom. So much maturity. I have so much admiration for this young Black couple that is defying all of society's negative expectations.

Malik, 25, and Bri, 24, are continuously learning and growing within their partnership of husband and wife. Not very many of us have peers who are married in their early twenties, so the examples we have are usually our elders or our parents. Malik and Bri each come from what they called "broken homes," yet they made it their business to blaze a new trail and take a chance on the love they're sure they have for each other. Bri recalled what she witnessed while growing up between her mother and father:

"My parents argued and ended up getting divorced. Honestly, it affected me in a positive way. I just saw what my parents had, and I knew I didn't want that. So I became very specific in terms of what I wanted.

"I don't want to speak for Malik, but we both came from broken homes, and we both realized divorce was seen as a norm to everyone else. But Malik and I decided divorce is not normal, and we wanted something different."

Malik, agreeing with his wife, added to what she was saying. What he saw between his parents made him yearn for something better:

"I'm negatively motivated. There was a lot of fights between my parents. There was a lot of love too—don't get me wrong. But they weren't on the same page. They had different goals. Maybe they had the same goals, and they just went about them in different ways."

Malik said his parents' differences led to his father going his separate way from the family.

His father's absence influenced Malik to learn about provision and being the man of the house at a young age:

"Our house went up for bankruptcy, so me and my mom were homeless for a little while. My brother was in college, and my dad went and did his thing. So it was just me and my mom for the most part. I was a caddie at the time, and I worked in the sound room at our church, so I had these odd jobs. I was paying rent with tip money basically. I had to grow up and pay rent when I was thirteen."

With what little money Malik had, it's quite commendable of him to take on the duty of helping his mother any way he could during his adolescence. Perhaps this abrupt end to a responsibility-free childhood is what prepared his mind for manhood early on.

As a result, Bri sensed Malik's maturity and his humble upbringing in conjunction with his respect for the woman of the house back then, his mother. It undoubtedly groomed him for a successful marriage with Bri as she shares the same values and expectations as him:

"My definition of 'provision' is letting my man lead from the front. He leads the household. When you hear 'provision,' you think of financial aspects. But I also think of provision as my man providing that safe place. It's a financial thing but also security."

As stated before, Bri and Malik have consciously decided to take on traditional gender roles within their marriage. They've come to the agreement that these roles contribute to their harmonious relationship and mutual understanding.

"In our marriage, I believe she's supposed to trust me and love me. She still should have enough say in what goes on. However, if there's a decision that I have to make that I honestly feel is for her safety and in our best interest, then I'd say 'Hey, this is what I've decided we need to do. I just need you to trust me on this.' I appreciate her just allowing me to make those decisions."

While Bri submits, Malik also knows there's an expectation for him to provide a safe haven for his wife and be the head of the household, and he's more than willing to fulfill her needs.

"Provision all boils down to security. Being able to contribute to her peace of mind and let her know that as far as the household is concerned, things are taken care of; making sure she comes to a home where she can be safe and secure—it doesn't have a price tag on it. It has a lot to do with how attentive you are to detail—paying attention to her concerns and giving her what she needs."

After Malik finished his definition of proper provision, when Bri was presented with the same question, she laughed before saying, "He stole my answer."

That, to me, is a sure sign that they are both on the same page and thus headed in the right direction—toward an everlasting union.

When Bri explained her desire to be submissive to her husband, she also disclosed how this decision wouldn't sit well with a few of her friends. Bri feels this modern age of extreme feminists—some of whom are categorizing themselves as "independent" women—believe it's a shame for Bri to want to be submissive.

"If I were to go tell my friends that I'm submissive to my husband, which I am, they'd be like 'Uh, I'm an independent woman. I don't need a man'—as if I don't do anything for myself. I don't know why it's seen as such a negative thing—as if it means you always wait on your husband hand and foot—almost like you're a slave."

But according to Bri, this is a negative connotation that mainly circulates heavily within the African American community. She feels there's a different perception of provision when speaking in terms of White couples.

"People see a White woman submitting to her husband and assume 'Oh, that's them. That's their culture.' But I feel it should be standard in everyone's relationship that the wife is submissive to her husband."

Even if this is true and it would benefit us more to stand firm on these traditional gender norms, submission doesn't stand a chance if it depends on a man's capability to provide and the perception of provision is way off. She feels Black women specifically may be expecting an unrealistic form of provision. Perhaps it's the idolization of famous Black couples or just the need to try to keep up with their friends and what they're able to afford. Either way, it's further perpetuating romantically destructive ideologies.

"A lot of Black women think all the material things given to them are what makes a man a provider. Some of them think 'He's gonna buy me this bag or these shoes,' and that's not always the case. A lot of Black women have that false perception, thinking that's what the whole relationship is gonna be like."

Thus, those same people who don't have the right understanding of provision breathe more life into the whole "Black men don't provide" narrative. Sometimes—when it comes down to it—"Black men don't provide" is code for "My Black man won't buy me everything I want."

And that's unfortunate, considering the fact that Black men gain an automatic disadvantage if they're not as rich as the couples on Instagram make themselves out to be. Black men especially are put under an obscene amount of pressure and unfairly scrutinized.

"I think the way they judge them is pretty clear-cut, but it's limiting. I believe they judge Black men off their position but not their potential. There are men striving for more, and they want more, but they don't have much to show for."

Then Malik came to another realization: if a husband feels he's not in a desirable or valuable position in life, it leads to discontent in the marriage. It makes matter worse when he has to put up with everyone else's input and judgement based off his level of "provision" instead of the amount of genuine love and respect he has for his woman. It can become exhausting.

"For me, if I weren't where I am at right now mentally, to be honest with you, it would suck. It would be like, 'Dude, I have to take care of myself, and I have to take care of her.' The first thing I'd be thinking about if we go out to eat is 'I have two bills instead of one.' Resentment would start to build up, and I'd be like, 'Who's gonna take care of me? It's not fair.' You have to be careful not to get to that point because now you're resenting her."

Resentment can tear apart two people who had the best intentions all because they lacked communication and teamwork. Sharing the same goals and dreams as your partner and working toward them together—no matter what that may look like—should always be the main objective.

"Malik and I run a business together, so there are decisions that I make and decisions that he makes, but as I said, I let him lead from the front. Still, I am right behind him—on board with the plan."

That's it right there. It's important for couples to never lose sight of their *plan*. Malik said that this is essentially what keeps a man on track—prioritizing his family's progression and protection:

"A man with a plan is really what women want. We need structure in life in general as humans—especially when it comes to relationships. So I feel like men need to focus more on their why. 'Why do I want to pursue whatever this is long-term? What do I want to get out of this, generationally speaking?' You know? What is your drive?

"I think when a man gets down to his why and it doesn't get lost in the sauce of social media, then he'll know why he gets up every morning and provides for his wife—because she deserves it and because he loves her."

Malik and Bri, ladies and gentlemen.

Enough said.

Chapter 18

Fletcher and Carol—The Seasoned Love

"She's robbing the cradle!" Fletcher, 59, laughed as he joked about his and Carol's age difference.

But don't be misled; Carol's the most subtly sexy sixty-five-year-old woman anyone could ever have the pleasure of meeting. She's even mastered the art of making hard work look good—with a thriving career as an entrepreneur and successful saleswoman *dominating* the makeup industry.

Carol's showing no signs of slowing down.

Her husband had to catch her while he could. Though she's fabulously stunning, she's still classy and graceful. But out of all her attributes, she says she's a woman of God first and foremost.

After being divorced for several years, Carol took pride in how self-sufficient and ambitious she was—all while being a great mother to her son and daughter, who are now thriving adults themselves.

Her husband, on the other hand, is a skilled and super talented independent contractor. Fletcher, being the visionary he is, transforms old, falling-apart properties into dream homes you'd have to see to believe.

Together, the two of them are moneymaking go-getters, both bringing plentiful proceeds to the table.

Carol said she knew it would take a strong man like Fletcher to prove to her that he was a suitable leader—and that, he did.

However, before they said their "I dos," Carol said that she wanted to stay true to her godly grounding; her mother's words and teachings stayed in her heart.

While some might say that provision and submission applies as boyfriend and girlfriend pretty much the same as husband and wife, Carol expressed and supported her opposing view.

"I'm not trusting somebody who doesn't think I'm worthy of being his wife. I'm not submitting to someone who doesn't think I'm good enough to be his wife. The Word says that the wife is to submit to the husband. I ain't doin' all that submittin' if we're boyfriend and girlfriend. Nah, that's not the same thing."

I conducted the interview over the phone, and I could hear Fletcher mumbling and scoffing in disagreement. After listening to her reasoning, he declared, bluntly, "You might lose out that way too!"

Carol laughed with a sassy statement: "Oh, well, it worked out for *me* just fine."

She had a point! Fletcher respected her wishes and was proud to put a ring on it.

To submit or not to submit during the dating stage—that is the question.

It is a loaded question, in all honesty. At what point is the lack of provision or refusal of submission an indicator that the relationship isn't going anywhere?

Even as they disagreed, I could tell that it was still all love; they laughed and mocked each other for their opposing opinions. Fletcher had his turn to offer a rebuttal.

"I think it could work both ways [submission while dating and once you're married]. You're dating up to marriage. You should be for real with who you are leading up to marriage. There are a lot of relationships where a partner is one way, and then things change when they get married. I think you should start the relationship the way you wanna finish it."

And for many men and women like Fletcher, it's just that simple. If two people know they're dating exclusively and they're talking about marriage, they're doing everything else that married people do if you catch my drift.

But it's easy for people to pick and choose which roles they'd like to subscribe to and which ones they feel shouldn't apply—usually the ones that are less fun and require more understanding and discipline and putting yourself in your partner's shoes.

"Fletcher knows, when we were dating, there were just certain things I wasn't comfortable doing, especially in front of my kids. So I was holding back a little because we weren't married! I hear what he's saying. Some guys might not be willing to wait. But 'to thine own self be true.' That's how my mother raised me. So I had to stick to my values, and I took my chances."

At this point, Fletcher shot back jokingly, "You gotta go through boot camp!"

During the interview, he was a man of few words, but there were still some points that he made *sure* he got out in the open.

Hearing Carol and Fletcher banter back and forth cracked me up. But on a serious note, I loved how genuine this couple was. They brought up a thought-provoking outlook that I hadn't even pondered. When we were discussing the way society talks about and interacts with Black men versus Black women, Carol shared some interesting food for thought.

"Not blaming institutionalism, but it is a fact that society has always been more comfortable elevating the Black woman, and I think they've done that intentionally to be very divisive within the Black family."

In all honesty, I never thought of it this way. Could it really be that society feels that the Black man and the Black woman are a powerful force to be reckoned with, and they don't even realize it because they've been brainwashed to the point where they see each other as the enemy?

Creating such a dynamic duo could be downright intimidating— the key to the next revolution that they hope to never bear witness to. So the media instigates the tension that Black people already have accumulated over the years due to our troublesome past and uses it to uplift our women as a way to make them look at the Black man in pity? Creating animosity between Black women and Black men could possibly be a foolproof way to keep us divided.

"The more independent the Black woman becomes, and as the media talks about how she's become more or just as financially stable as the Black man, the more divisive it is to our relationships. And it brings this sense of arrogance that says 'I don't need you. What do I need you for? I can do this for myself.'"

Generational wealth and security don't stem from a "What can you do for me?" attitude; they stem from an "Imagine all that we can accomplish together" mindset.

Massive success as a couple comes from being wise enough to invest your monies properly with the help of financial professionals. It comes from contributions made from each other's hard work. It comes from building an empire.

Carol understands that there are Black women who can not only "bring something to the table," so to speak, but they can also buy that same table two times over and fill them both with all the fixings she sees fit.

However, Carol is also aware of those women who have long lists of expectations for their men but can hardly do anything for themselves.

In terms of how people verbalize their expectations regarding submission versus provision, Carol said she often sees women on social media vocalize their anticipations and opinions.

"Personally, I see more women do it than men. I see more women get on social media, talking about 'This nigga's gonna have to be able to buy this, and he better to do this. He gone have to put rocks on my hands'—you know? They say all that craziness, and then I go and look at her profile, and she doesn't have two dimes to rub together herself! Yet she expects to attract that?

"They have been misinformed. I know guys have their perceptions. I just don't see them post it as much. They just don't seem to be as vocal about it. I guess theirs is more implied."

The bottom line is, you cannot invest and build with someone you don't trust—with someone you don't actually see as your partner.

Part 3

Strong Women and Submission

Chapter 19

The Interconnectedness of Success, Provision, and Submission According To God's Word

When it's all said and done (as cliché as that may sound), we must realize that we have been in the dark for much too long. Pointing fingers, making demands, and being contentious with one another hasn't gotten us anything but trending topics on social media. For what it's worth, I'd say I expected much better from millennials, the alleged "most advanced" generation there is.

One thing Katrina said during her interview (well, after the recorder was turned off) really stuck with me: "People are rooted in the world, not rooted in the Word."

The Word, or the Bible, was described as an acronym when I was a kid in Sunday school: Basic Instructions Before Leaving Earth. However, what Katrina was getting at was how our priorities do away with God's Word or his "instructions." Instead, it seems we've traded the Bible for that little blue app—the Book—or that little purple app—the Gram. Our relationship role models and the people we hold to such high standards and put on pedestals are not always worthy examples of how we should conduct ourselves romantically.

My last interview subject, First Lady Maureen, said it plainly:

"I believe that today, if people look to the media for examples of a solid foundation for marriage, then they are in sinking sand

because the media isn't designed to take you to the kingdom. It's designed for you to fail here on earth."

Prior to her role as the preacher's wife at her and her husband's church, First Lady Maureen, 62, was an administrative leader for a noteworthy Missouri school district and the principal of a school in Florida for seventeen years. She also served as a minister of education for a government office in China.

"I was in China for about four and a half years before Pastor came along and said, 'Come home and marry me.' I didn't wanna come back to Saint Louis. I liked the warm weather. But for him, I made the sacrifice. I submitted."

She laughed a sweet laugh, almost blushing at the thought of her husband. A gentle-spirited woman, she spoke calmly and kindly, but her words carried such weight and truth.

These days, as a retired educator and an honorable woman of God, First Lady Maureen facilitates marriage counseling as one of her ministries in the church.

She said that the biggest pain point is none other than the topic of submission.

"I've done a lot of marriages in the last four years, and 'submission' always comes up in marital counseling. That's a word we spend almost a whole session on. But the views they bring to the marriage counseling are different than the views they take away from the marriage counseling. It is not about hierarchy, and unfortunately, that's their mindset when they come in."

Traditional wedding vows reference Ephesians 5:21–24: "Submit to one another out of reverence of Christ. Wives submit to your husbands as you do to the Lord. For the husband is the head of the wife, as Christ is the head of the church, His body, of which He is the savior. Now as the church submits to Christ, so also wives should submit to their husbands in everything."

Whew! Those are some straightforward guidelines directly from the Bible.

But First Lady Maureen said that lots of couples are removing the word "submit" from their vows altogether—traditional or otherwise.

"I've even seen young couples getting married, and they will not use the word 'submission' in their vows. They rewrite them so that word no longer exists. When I see things like that happening, that tells me they don't have a true understanding of what submission is in the eyes of God."

While not all of us are called to marry a dignified leader of a place of worship, some find it unsettling, or they feel too vulnerable if they submit, essentially leaving their fate and their destiny in the hands of another. No matter how much we may love and adore someone, lots of us struggle with trust.

"'Submission' becomes a negative word when you're not submitting to the right one and when you don't have God at the center of it. And, unfortunately, that is why a lot of our marriages are falling by the wayside. They don't have a solid foundation, which is the Word of God."

As for First Lady Maureen, submission may almost seem as if it's second nature to her. As she said earlier, when Pastor asked for her hand in marriage, she completed her assignment abroad and came back home to be with the one she loved. She submitted. She made it sound much easier than what our generation makes it out to be. And now that they've been married for years, her outlook on the role of a husband is simple:

"He is going to oversee the house, the wife, the kids. He's going to be my right hand. He's going to be the one who creates a safe environment that I can thrive in—not so I can be told what to do and how to do but to become all that I can be in the marriage. The provider is not a person that dictates. He engages. He communicates. And for me, he's someone that is connected—aligned with the Word."

First Lady Maureen is living proof of how one can enjoy the best of both worlds; she was living out her dreams and fulfilling the purpose that God had for her life and still found love in his perfect time.

But, as I stated earlier, some of us are apprehensive about how we should proceed in life—whether we're single or married. We have the desire to spread our wings and be all that we can be, but at the same time, we're unsure of where our ambitions may land us. Successful and alone? Or in a relationship and unfulfilled personally and spiritually?

We tend to worry so much, and anxiety takes a toll on our relationships and kills our peace of mind. Even though it's spelled out plainly in the Word of God, we still tend to stress, believing we can overwork ourselves into contentment and happiness. But actually, in doing so, we are robbing ourselves of those things and so much more.

Psalm 37:4 says, "Take delight in the Lord, and He will give you the desires of your heart."

Matthew 6:25–27 says, "Therefore I tell you, do not worry about your life, what you will eat or drink; or about your body, what you will wear. Is not life more than food, and the body more than clothes? Look at the birds in the air; they do not sow or reap or store away in barns, and yet, your heavenly Father feeds them. Are you not much more valuable than they? Can any one of you by worrying add a single hour to your life?"

Matthew 6:33 says, "But seek first His kingdom, and His righteousness and all these things will be given to you as well."

Essentially, if we were rooted in the Word, instead of allowing social media to have so much dominion over our lives, we'd realize how blessed we are and how blessed God plans for us to be.

First Lady Maureen said she tries to encourage the members of her ministry.

"Today, I tell those young ladies in a minute, 'Get in the Word. Understand what it says. Don't put your blessings in the layaway when you can get 'em today.'"

First ladies are highly regarded and respected within their communities and organizations. While most of that respect seemingly stems from simply being married to the man in charge, there are multiple achievements, certifications, and positions that many first women have earned prior to them being married to prominent men in power.

Aside from First Lady Maureen, another perfect example is former First Lady Michelle Obama.

Michelle earned two degrees from prestigious establishments: one from Princeton, an Ivy League school, and another one from Harvard Law School. This made Michelle and Hillary Clinton, her fellow former first lady who graduated from Wellesley College, the highest educated first ladies in American history.

Soon after Michelle became the vice president of community and external affairs for the University of Chicago Medical Center, her husband, Barack, announced his candidacy for the 2008 Democratic presidential nomination.

Although Michelle loved her leadership role at the University of Chicago, she decided to take leave from her position to fully devote herself to her husband's vision. After all was said and done, he led not only the Obama family but the entire world into a historical phenomenon—America seeing the first African American president of the United States.

It's true—Barack Obama blazed his own trail as an unfairly scrutinized yet beloved commander in chief. All the while, the world was getting to know Michelle. As we watched her take a pay cut and do away with her obligations at her own job to take care of their two young girls while Obama worked tirelessly to win the presidential campaign, it endeared her to many.

In 2020, Michelle was named the most admired woman for the third year straight.

Barack credits his wife's love, her belief in him, and her support for his many successes in life. He became all that he could be because of their combined strength; they were better together. She used her knowledge, her education, and her voice to uplift Barack spiritually and mentally during his campaign and both terms of his presidency.

Michelle trusted Barack to bring about positive change in America and to improve their personal lives; therefore, she felt safe in her submission to him.

Needless to say, Barack Obama wasn't half-stepping on his duty to provide either. He protected his wife and their daughters. He publicly showed adoration and appreciation for them and led them to an even higher and more comfortable place than before.

Barack exceeded his due diligence as a provider and continues to do so, according to Michelle's best-selling memoir and her Netflix special, *Becoming*.

And any woman who is willing to submit should expect nothing less.

No, I'm not saying that your partner needs to be famous, extremely wealthy, or become the next president of the United States. Don't miss my point; your partner only needs to always have your best interests at heart. Their vision needs to be clear. They need to be intentional and consistent in their actions from day one. Their mind should be focused on God, elevation, and progression. And most importantly, they need to be making sure that you receive the love and appreciation you deserve.

Submission is great, but it needs to be given wisely.

Submission isn't free; it must be earned based on your demonstrations as a worthy leader.

Yes, submission takes tears and grit. For a lot of women, it takes many sacrifices. But if he's the one, he'll prove himself if you give him the chance, and he'll make it all worth your while.

Choosing a man who is worthy of your submission is a prerequisite to a godly marriage.

"Because of your desire to want and not to be, you want everything you see, but your desire is not to be everything God has planned for you to be."

Chapter 20

Submission Is Not for the Weak

It's crazy what can cause controversy these days.

My favorite Pastor, Steven Furtick, once preached a sermon called "The Prison of Offense," where he asked his congregation, "Have you noticed we live in an age of perpetual offense?" He then talked about how everybody is offended about everything all the time. He even jokingly told the church about how he must pray for twenty minutes before he posts something on his social media just to provide an extra layer of God's protection against accidentally offending someone.

Regular people say things on their social media every day, and people who have nothing better to do will sit and go back and forth with them about their opposing beliefs.

But the offense intensifies when a prominent figure or a celebrity publicly voices their opinion. People are enraged by their points of view or their beliefs, then reporters and gossip columnists all rush to tell us how they're "catching backlash" from their recent revelations.

Well, imagine catching backlash for wanting to be submissive to your husband.

Jeannie Mai is an Emmy- and NAACP-winning daytime talk show host, entertainer, and producer.

Yesterday, she made headlines for tying the knot with hip hop artist and entrepreneur Jay "Jeezy" Jenkins.

However, just last year, when the couple was still engaged, Jeannie made headlines for a different reason—she was criticized by fans after she expressed her plan to be submissive to Jeezy during an episode of *The Real.*

The fact that her comments were immediately labeled as controversial gave me pause.

"Controversial" is defined as "giving rise or likely to give rise to public disagreement."

"Controversial" is synonymous with "problematic" and "contentious."

What Jeannie said was, "Going into my marriage, I want to submit to my man."

And people viewed *that* as problematic.

People had contentious feelings toward *that* statement.

Almost immediately after she said this, before she could even get another word out, looks of shock, confusion, or indifference spread across her cohosts' faces.

Jennie proceeded with her explanation:

"I'm a very dominant woman. I own my business. I lead my teams. I played my own manager, my own publicist, and my own lawyer when I didn't have money to have those people. So I make the decisions in my life. When I come home, I like the idea that my man leads us."

While it's true that Jeannie received a lot of flak for her decision to submit, she also received lots of praise. Some professionals even came to her defense, backing up her comments with logic and critical thinking that support her reasoning for submission.

During a discussion on *PIX11 News*, licensed marriage and family therapist Dr. Lexx Brown-James gave some of her input:

"Women—really specifically marginalized women—are taught to accrue power. They have to be the boss. They have to get an education. They have to make the money. They have to make decisions for community, family, children, parents, grandparents, church, and a lot of that leads to decision fatigue.

"So coming home to a lover, who you trust and who you're willing to be vulnerable with, you're able to lay down those decisions and say, 'I'm good. I feel safe with you. I can trust you to make the decisions for our household

because I'm tired. I don't want to think about another "yes" or another "no" or another "maybe"—another "go.""

In another interview with *Us Weekly*, Jeannie gave more wisdom and insight on her decision:

"I am more of a powerful woman because I understand my power of choice and that I would like to appreciate my man's role by giving him the ability to make decisions for us. That doesn't mean he doesn't factor in my thoughts and my wishes. That doesn't mean that I'm any less equal than him. It means that I'm saying, 'I trust you.'

"I have to allow him to be the framework in our marriage and in our life. And he knows enough to ask me questions to incorporate what I want to build the vision for us together."

Jennie Mai isn't the only celebrity who's become known for her choice to submit to her husband. Fantasia Barrino is a vocal powerhouse who rose to fame after she won the third season of *American Idol*.

No stranger to publicity—good and bad—the singer has experienced the best and worst of the media. Fantasia continues to evolve over the years even after the trauma she's endured. She's lived through the whirlwind of emotions she experienced because of the antagonizing of the media.

Fantasia's Lifetime movie revealed how her relationship with her daughter's father was toxic and abusive. These days, several years later, Fantasia publicly thanks God for her newfound love—her husband of over six years, Kendall Taylor.

Next thing you know, *her critics* publicly *shamed* her after an interview she had with the award-winning radio show *The Breakfast Club*. The interview was so controversial, it went viral. Fantasia's following sentiments rubbed some listeners the wrong way:

"Most women are trying to be the leader. That's why you can't find a man. You can't be the king in the house. Fall back and be the queen and let your man lead the way. At the end of the day, I'm the neck. My man's the head."

Fantasia's fans are used to her and her husband's openness and transparency in terms of the dynamic of their relationship.

As a matter of fact, the songstress and her husband host Facebook and Instagram livestreams called *Taylor Talks Live with Fantasia and Kendall*.

A few topics they often discuss include gender roles, submission, and provision.

One of their candid conversations made waves as well when they posted a video regarding submission.

Kendall expressed how he feels submission should be between husband and wife:

"So here's the issue: Submission is supposed to be a beautiful song and dance between two lovers. What's happened is, men have abused that gift. We have been misled to think that it's a dominant spirit. That we own decisions, we dictate everything, we rule with an iron fist. First of all, that's not love. What happens in my marriage is, I submit daily to the Most High. I stay in my scriptures. I continue to feed myself with things that help me build my character to reshape my perspective."

His points remind me of Colossians 3:19: "Husbands, love your wives, and do not be harsh with them."

Kendall's comments were a full-circle moment that brought me back to what First Lady Maureen told me regarding both husband and wife staying rooted in the Word to maintain a strong foundation within marriage.

"Because I know what the Word says about submission, it flows. In order to be in line with blessings, I have to accept what the Word says about submission."

I couldn't help but realize that noteworthy women like Jeannie Mai, Fantasia, and Michelle Obama are pretty similar to First Lady Maureen in terms of the ideology of submission.

The only difference is three of them are famous and First Lady Maureen is not.

But on the same token, they were already powerful, successful, and accomplished women before and after they met their loved ones and gracefully decided to submit to them.

In other words, it's time for our generation to come to this realization: "Submission" isn't synonymous with "weak."

But healthy and mindful submission *is* synonymous with "substantial," "solid," and "strong."

Chapter 21

In Conclusion

Now that we've taken in data, information, and all these opinions, what's next?

Let me suggest a thorough self-examination.

We all have fears. We've all endured various degrees of trauma. We have flaws. Everyone is difficult in one way or another.

But that doesn't mean that any one of us is unworthy of love and protection.

There are things that we can't control, such as the events of the past and how certain misfortunes left some of us emotionally scarred or overly defensive and callous.

My hope is for us to focus on what we *can* control—being intentional in our romantic relationships and developing an understanding of how to lovingly submit and how to dutifully provide and do each with humility and the purest intentions.

With that being said, I also hope we've learned a lot about ourselves after considering these interviews and statistics and the information presented with evidence and merit.

It's time that we stop blaming the system, the privilege of our White brothers and sisters, or upbringings filled with unfit, undereducated, or undignified examples. Instead, we need to take full responsibility for being vocal about what we want, what we need, and what we expect—not in terms of tangible or material things but in terms of the heart, mind, body, and spirit.

God doesn't have any favorites. There's enough success, wealth, peace, and joy for us all—whether it's our season to enjoy those gifts alone or share them with the ones we love.

Provision and submission are just two of the gazillion key factors of every relationship. That means that you and your partner must decide, based off your unique situation, what would be the best, most honorable dynamic between the two of you in the sight of God.

I'm no expert on successful relationships; if that were the case, I'd at least be happily married by now myself. But my passion for the topics of love and relationships has compelled me to dive deep into the sea of uncertainty. I enjoyed fleshing out people's ideas and charging forward to a better understanding for myself that I can maybe share with others.

And with that, I'll leave you with these final words from Ephesians 3:14–19 (NIV):

"For this reason, I kneel before the father, from whom every family in heaven and on earth derives its name. I pray that out of His glorious riches He may strengthen you with His power, through His spirit in your inner being, so that Christ may dwell in your hearts through faith. And I pray that you, being rooted, and established in love, may have power together with all the Lord's holy people, to grasp how high and long and wide and deep is the love of Christ, and to know this love that surpasses knowledge—that you may be filled to the measure of all the fullness of God."

Sources

The Prison of Offense | The Other Half | Pastor Steven Furtick - YouTube

Michelle Obama | Biography & Facts | Britannica

Michelle Obama named most admired woman for third straight year: poll | TheHill

Fantasia Gets Backlash For Saying Women Need To 'Submit' | NewsOne

Unpacking Jeannie Mai's comments on submitting to her man - YouTube

The Wealth of Generations, With Special Attention to the Millennials | NBER

No More FOMO: Limiting Social Media Decreases Loneliness and Depression | Journal of Social and Clinical Psychology (guilfordjournals. com)

How Many People Use Social Media in 2021? (65+ Statistics) (backlinko. com)

Conventions of Courtship: Gender and Race Differences in the Significance of Dating Rituals (nih.gov)

The Complete History of Social Media: Then And Now - Small Business Trends (smallbiztrends.com)